MW01623936

Death by Saxophone

Debbie Burke

Death by Saxophone

Published by Queen Esther Publishing LLC
ISBN 978-1-7362216-5-5

Edited by Calen Nakash
Cover art by Charlie Coatney
Graphic design by Donna Lynn/Bruce Hall

AUTHOR'S NOTE

Several years ago, I came across an article published by NPR about the mysterious Cold War "bone records" and was immediately struck by its potential for a jazz noir novel. The what-ifs jumped out at me: imagine a story about owning something so rare and (let's say) dangerous that it caused the demise of one very wealthy and entitled saxophone musician. To make things more complicated, what if he was a beloved entertainer to some, but reviled by others...and had a few enemies, to boot?

In this book, I've drawn on my many jazz experiences, from playing the saxophone in local bands to writing a popular jazz blog to writing fiction and nonfiction books on jazz and other music. By the way, I have strong ties to the Verrazano Bridge (on the cover). I was there at the ribbon-cutting.

So, what of our anti-hero?

Now you can find out what happens to such a man.

Debbie Burke

To Richie, Rachel and Tim:

the three parts of my heart

We take the cool neck
of this music, cradle in our fingers
its body: a shape without edges
which pulses in time to the ways
we are desperate to move.

Oh how we beg to be
ever-submerged in the honey
that drips from each note.

–Zoe Branch/*flora & phrase*

Death by Saxophone

PROLOGUE

Rebecca ("Becka") Rifkin would never forget where she was when she found out that sax musician Jerry Zolotov fell off the Verrazano Bridge.

She was on the Verrazano Bridge.

Normally, this would have been something she heard about through the internet, where anything momentarily deemed news spread like flames licking paper, bringing social destruction to every corner it reached. But here she was, directly affected by the terrible news.

Her mother had just died, and she needed to set her mom's affairs in order. Her last place of residence was a small apartment at Staten Island's Moonglow Assisted Living. The bereavement policy at the hospital where Becka worked on MRI machines was generous. She fully intended to take all five days.

Becka had a complicated relationship with her mother, but the good news was that with therapy (her own), they'd come to an unspoken agreement that had provided peace and release. There was a slim period where they weren't at each other's throats, so her visits to Moonglow went smoothly, without that crackling sense of dread that made her neck throb. One month after learning how to navigate their repartee without hate and resentment, her mom was gone. Now, tying up loose ends in Staten Island, Becka looked through her mom's belongings, bagged most of the clothing for donation and said teary goodbyes to the staff. The day was winding down and she was bone tired. She picked up some Jewish deli for the ride home.

The November sun had just sunk below the horizon and she was on the road by six p.m. The drive back to her place in Brighton Beach would normally take just minutes on the Verrazano and then onto the Belt Parkway, which ultimately circled the southeast end of Brooklyn. But when the bridge swung into view, she saw one lane closed off and police cars chunked all over the eastbound side. Her side.

She hated driving when it was dark and called her best friend, Lizzy McCaffrey, for company.

"What the—?" she mumbled between bites of turkey on seeded rye with Russian dressing and only a *bisl* of coleslaw. "I wonder what the heck happened here!" she said to her friend.

Lizzy was putting her kids to sleep. Becka could hear them whining and stalling. They were pretty good kids, but they weren't tired yet and needed to be convinced of that fact. Lizzy did a good job setting down the law.

"Listen to this!" Lizzy said. "I'm on Twitter. There's some really big holdup on the bridge. Not that you have an alternative, unless you want to go back up into Manhattan and...."

"Damn! The cops are all over the place. Wait! Cool! They're letting me go through." Becka rubbernecked to get a better view of the scenery but couldn't tell what was going on. She had to keep her eyes on the road.

"What are they saying?" she asked Lizzy. "God forbid it's a jumper. I don't see anything that looks like a crash."

"Um, it's pretty bad. Be careful driving."

"What is it?" Becka had a caraway seed stuck in her teeth but she kept both hands on the wheel. Traffic cones were all over the place.

"Gotta love the Courier. 'Smooth jazz icon's last gig: Jerry Zolotov's body found off NYC bridge.'"

"No shit! When did this happen?"

"Overnight last night. Like 3 a.m."

"And the cops are still here? There's yellow tape all over the place."

Becka had been a jazz fan since about third grade. Before he died, her dad played lots of Wayne Shorter and Johnny Hodges and Sinatra at home. He never got to hear what became known as smooth jazz, and good thing. He would have dismissed it out of hand. Only the originals for him; he could be a bit of a snob that way.

In the '70s, when her college friends were heading to the clubs to overdress for the last days of disco, Becka was scouring the subterranean holes-in-the-wall for jazz, and now she was glad she did. She got to see some of the stalwarts that failed to make it through the '80s. When she first heard smooth jazz on CD 101.9 in New York City, she was about to toss it out the window but decided to give it a chance. It grew on her, big-time. It wasn't as complex as straight-ahead (or mainstream) jazz, but it was stress-free. You didn't have to think about what you were hearing: strong melodies, unadorned harmonies and a simple rhythmic structure.

Becka had not only heard of Jerry Zolotov, she'd become a fan. She refused to feel ashamed, either. There was room in the world for both kinds of jazz without anyone having to apologize for it.

Over the past few months, she'd been angling to bring her mother to one of his shows. When it was announced he was going to perform at Staten Island Lowe's Theater, it would be a cinch to figure out the logistics, signing her out of Moonglow for a few hours for a night out that they would both always remember. Something told Becka it would be one of the last things they would do together, but she had dragged her feet getting tickets (her therapist could help her figure out why) and the date had come and gone.

Now all she had was a turkey sandwich all over her lap and questions about how Jerry Zolotov met his demise.

There was joy in the DuPont household when Rozina got the job as the personal assistant for Jerry Zolotov. She couldn't believe she would be working with the hottest saxophone player around.

"Watch how you use the word 'hot,'" her husband, Eric DuPont, teased her.

"Don't worry, and I mean it. I find him kind of self-important and a show-off. Besides, I'm madly in love with another man. You might know him."

Eric got up from the breakfast table to hug his wife. He kissed the top of her head.

"Now we'll be able to afford the right shoes for you."

Rozina sighed. "Thank God. These ugly ones are a throwback to 1952. I can't wait to get something pretty for once."

Being born with an inverted right foot and a femur that was two inches shorter than her left one was a challenge to deal with, especially in Phys Ed. The teachers made her sit it out, but she hated being excluded.

Her parents got her a second-hand orthopedic shoe that didn't fit right. It was painful, but she smiled through it and found a way to run with the other kids and participate in most of the sports activities. She wouldn't let it determine her life course or how she thought of herself. "It's just something I put on, like my socks. It's just another part of getting dressed."

Her parents were proud of her positive attitude but knew that she was a lonely child. The pig-tailed little girl next door was her only friend. All the other kids laughed at her and pretended to limp around in the schoolyard. The girls were worse than the boys. When it came time for the high school prom, she was shocked that one young man asked her out. She'd not noticed him before but then remembered he was in her math class. "I love how you go up to the board and solve equations like they were nothing," he said. It was the best pickup line she'd ever heard. "May I please take you to prom?"

Rozina smiled at the memory. And now Eric was peering at her from over his newspaper, getting ready to have his scrambled eggs. "What's up, buttercup?"

"Just thankful, that's all."

He blew her a kiss. "You deserve all the good things. What will you be doing for Jerry, anyway?"

"Oh, you know. Phone calls, bookings, writing press releases, all of it. People say he's a tyrant but I've worked with the toughest. Remember Mr. Klein, my boss at Tidal Records? Now that was a grump."

Eric nodded heartily. "So this Jerry guy, he plays smooth jazz? Please! He's gonna be a pushover."

♪

They say that once a century, a savant so astounding emerges who turns the performing arts field upside down and inside out. In the smooth jazz world, it happened to be Jerzy Zolotov, otherwise known by his stage persona "Jerry Z."

Jerry felt that the path to success was not about being overly friendly so much as it was about keeping up appearances for his adoring fans, giving a high-energy show, and having the right administrative assistant behind the scenes.

"Roz!"

It was a muggy afternoon in Manhattan Beach. The smell of fish had wafted several blocks to Jerry's house. No amount of square footage or cathedral ceilings could keep it from coming in.

He'd built the house back in 1979, when home prices were not yet stratospheric in the Borough of Churches, as Brooklyn was called. The only thing his former manager got right was how the neighborhood would go up in value.

The move from Astoria, Queens, made sense. His new home sat on an acre and a half just a block away from Manhattan Beach. There was some mob activity, or so he'd heard, but Jerry had a good security team and was careful whom he rubbed elbows with, not taking favors and therefore not owing favors. With his new assistant Rozina DuPont coming on board soon and a new PR person, he could start the next phase of his career.

He loved the idea of a subterranean studio. As soon as the home was christened with some high-end bourbon and a few ladies who were occasional "visitors," the new sound studio could be built. The floating flooring and lighting were in place, but there were tons of equipment that had to be installed and tested. The sound and production experts were due over in a week. Once they started, the project took months, and Jerry Z was an impatient man.

"Come come! This studio isn't going to build itself!"

It was lonely with nobody around to answer him.

Rozina DuPont was hired as Jerry's "secretary" after his manager, Frankus Taylor, forced him to get a personal assistant. "Don't fight me on this, Jerry," Frankus told him. "All the big acts have several PAs." After hearing what his competitors (which is how he viewed his musical peers) had, he knew his manager was onto something.

He found Rozina through a second cousin who was living in Queens. They were talking one evening as Jerry complained about losing his datebook. "I guess my manager is right. But she better not get in the way."

His fans loved her. Although she was supposed to stay deep in the background, anyone who wanted to get close to Jerry but wanted to avoid his manager (Taylor was nicknamed The Bear, and for good reason) found Rozina much more pleasant. This was certainly true, but Rozina was a quiet bear in her own way, fiercely guarding Jerry's time and space.

Jerry's biggest problem was that he surrounded himself with the best talent, not just musicians but his accountant, PR person, manager, bodyguard/security, and, of course, Rozina, but he refused to heed their warnings. His revenues were taking a nosedive. Concert sales were bottoming out, he wasn't getting new bookings and tours, and even the dependable but tiny drip of income from music streaming services was at an all-time low. Not only was the industry starting to change (more streaming events, online master classes and individual instruction), but the genre itself was experiencing growing pains. While "smooth jazz" on its own terms initially found a happy niche, taking pieces from New Age, R&B and "real" jazz, his genre's heyday was short. As jazz bloomed into fusion, world music and classic contemporary, smooth jazz was seen as a less exciting alternative.

After a few decades in the industry, nobody felt this more than Jerry, who was exactly the kind of musician to rest on his laurels and not create anything fresh. The Bear told him—implored him—to write new material or at least collaborate with one of the majors (TJ Philippe, for example, at which Jerry shouted, "That charlatan!"). Naturally, Jerry took offense at the whole conversation.

Strange thing about fame. On your way up, you suffer from imposter syndrome. And on the way down, if you're Jerry Zolotov, you go into denial. Nothing's your fault; you're tanking because of the people around you; you chose the wrong team.

Rozina heard him complaining about his image and the "competition" constantly. She stopped rolling her eyes and trying to reason with him. Why was he so pigheaded? If he hated it so much, why didn't he go learn how to drive a bus or something?

"The fans know nothing!" he'd sputter. "If they saw where I came from, they would know an original when they heard it. Nobody has my sound, my stage energy and my melodies. Nobody!"

Poor Rozina didn't need to see his face to know it was as crimson as the customary strawberry rhubarb pie he had a slice of before bedtime. She would never tell Frankus about these tirades, though; he would have a conniption and yell at her (of all people): "You go and tell him to write some new music, for God's sake! While he's at it, he needs to get out there and walk the audience and schmooze." Rozina just let him vent. One boss was more than enough.

"His personality is in the shitter," Frankus continued. "You know as well as I that he's completely to blame for his low numbers. If he doesn't mingle and play nice with the fans, nobody's gonna buy his songs or come out to see him anymore."

Clearly, Jerry needed a fresh focus. It came in the guise of coveting something obscure. When Jerry's uncle in Ukraine told him about a relative who sold rare jazz recordings made during the Cold War called "bone records"—at a time when Soviet citizens were not allowed to listen to American music and found an ingenious way to make bootleg recordings onto old X-ray films—Jerry knew he had to have one. As soon as he had the cash, he told everyone who would listen that he'd buy "the rarest one of all!"

Rather than working on his reputation or his repertoire, Jerry squandered his spare time dreaming of snagging his very own X-ray record. His uncle had mentioned that Jerry's second cousin Pavel seemed like the best candidate to make this dream come true, and Jerry began needling Pavel unmercifully. He would beg (intimidate) his poor cousin, who had much more to worry about than his spoiled American counterpart. Jerry wouldn't let go until he got what he wanted.

Rozina knew her boss's ongoing obsession was about something much more fundamental than a sixty-year-old record pressed into a piece of X-ray film. Jerry's newfound object of desire was a way to bury the issues in his life: fears about his career, for sure, but an even deeper pain, a baseline loneliness. He could barely look in the mirror and confront himself because it would be a hopeless, vacant stare looking back at him, a depressing and perpetual Möbius strip of aloneness.

What others read as vanity—from Rozina to his manager to the girl at the deli where he got his potato latkes, from his nieces and nephews and cousins who lived in nearby Little Odessa—was really self-loathing, hating himself for being unlovable.

Nothing, however, could have prepared Jerry for the Holy Grail of all bone records. Cousin Pavel emailed him about something that had just become available: an X-ray of the right arm, left wrist and all ten fingers that had been broken and belonged to a little girl whose father happened to be a tyrant named Joseph Stalin.

The yen for this particular artifact almost caused Jerry to have a psychotic break. He knew he could afford it, whatever the price tag might be. The victory of acquisition would be sweet and inevitably followed by the public display of said treasure through well-placed mentions by his PR team. He called it a team, but Jerry had only one guy on PR duty, David Migliori, hired as a favor to his neighbor from long ago when he called Queens his home. David would understand, thought Jerry. He would appreciate the merit—no, the absolute need—for the world to know Jerry Zolotov was the owner of one of the most elusive objects in the world of music. It would add to his aura of mystery.

David often tried to talk Jerry out of such showy pursuits. "You have three platinum albums from seven, eight years ago," he'd told Jerry. "We're trying to get more buzz around your new single. Why in God's name would you flaunt your wealth to your fans now?"

Jerry had nearly fired him over that, but realized he needed David and needed to keep to his Queens promise or there would be other trouble. He owed somebody in Kew Gardens a lot of money for some long-ago payola. Money that he'd rather spend now on a Russian bone record.

Pavel had the right connections and the perfect personality to help Jerry get his bone record. An affable, forgettable guy who kept a low profile, he happened to have a dark secret. At the risk of being exposed by his famous cousin if things went awry, he indulged Jerry and agreed to look into it for him. *The faster I'm rid of this transaction, the better,* he thought. Not surprisingly, it took very little time, thanks to Pavel's shadowy network of not-so-friendly small-time operatives. He passed along some exciting information he had received from an acquaintance. A guy he knew, an engineer from Lvov named Rostislav, told him he knew how to get his hands on an authentic X-ray record.

"You get that guy Rosti and tell him I need to know how to BUY IT ASAP!" Jerry loved using solid caps in his emails and was not averse to ordering Pavel (or anyone else) around. Knowing Pavel's little secret was an insurance policy that both men had fore-of-mind.

Dear Jerzy,

I will have to ask Rostislav very politely for that price. He will let me know soon. We should do nothing else until we hear back from him.

Then, if you would like to purchase it, he will send me the details. You'll have to pay my fee separately and then deal with Rosti's person all on your own. I am only your information channel. I will not put my family in danger by getting involved in any transactions. But you are probably aware of the risks of such contraband and already know that you are going to pay a high price.

Pavel

Jerry saw red. He could barely reply.

Pavel,

You know I don't care how much it is. I really don't!!!!!!!!!! Yes I will pay you directly but you need to find out how I am to WIRE THE CASH to your friend. I don't expect a delay from you. I KNOW you can help me very much on this front.

Jerzy

The record would have to be obtained in person, not through postal mail or by ship. Pavel knew that

Rostislav would charge mightily to personally retrieve it from his contact.

It was bad enough that the record wasn't for sale through the usual back door channels like the black market or the dark web. It was supposedly secreted in the wall of a storeroom on the outskirts of St. Petersburg. Quiet rumors said that the room was lined with a special aluminum alloy baked into a ceramic cover that made it impervious to detection by drones, ultrasound or other photographic technology. Pavel didn't even want Rostislav to tell him where it came from. The less he knew, the better. He was only brokering the brokering of the deal. And naturally, since he'd done a little neck-sticking-out already, Jerry shouldn't mind paying an extra fee on top of it all, Pavel mused.

Soon enough, Pavel considered back-pedaling. He made the mistake of telling his wife, whom he loved more than life itself; a mistake because she wouldn't only try to talk him out of it but would also freak out. How much more should he tell her? The worry, the haranguing, figuring out what details he should be hiding from his wife. Was it even worth the payoff?

But Jerry's brand of insistence bordered on the malignant, and he went so far as to threaten Pavel with letting go of the one secret his cousin would hold till his grave, an extremely unfortunate one-night stand with an underage girl many years ago, which, naturally, Pavel's wife had no idea about (talk about freaking out; there would be a homicide). Pavel realized there was no backing out at this point. He was terrified that his crime would come to light. So he put on a cheery façade and plowed straight through it, determined to connect Rosti and Jerry together as soon as possible, then collect Jerry's fee and be done with it.

Jerry sent a two-character email to his cousin: $? to which Pavel replied: *$2.7M for R, $75K for me.* At least Jerry knew what he had to do. Scraping this together would take him no time at all.

Pavel could have even asked for more, the fool! Jerry thought. He'd have to tell Frankus and his accountant, Cathy Ann Hill.

Rostislav didn't know anything about Pavel's buyer or the family back story, nor did he need to. All that mattered was that the buyer had the funds to cover it. No surprise, the $2.7 mil was slightly higher than Rostislav had quoted, and when he asked Pavel about it, it was explained that it included a small fee for himself. Pavel may have been weak, but he was no pushover and had added this extra in as a "tip." His wife, however, still complained it was too little, calling her cousin-in-law a "cheapskate bastard who never helped us out when he got famous." Pavel knew it was more than a status symbol for Jerry; it was an affirmation, and he would pay the full price without balking.

Jerry sat on Pavel's neck every single week to nag him about it, and his cousin always replied patiently. "This takes time, Jerzy. You'll get it. Don't you think I want to be done with you?" He was only half-kidding.

Within four weeks, the money went from Jerry to Pavel and into Rostislav's dirty little paws. Three weeks from that, the payment was "processed" (whatever that meant) by the shipper. Then it went to Rosti and directly out to Brooklyn, New York, USA. After six more painful weeks in which Pavel's wife almost divorced him, Jerry confirmed he had picked it up from the post office. He was shocked at how small it was. Suspiciously small.

"These are the X-rays of an infant. What did you expect?" Pavel asked him.

"Well, thank you, cousin. Just remember what side your bread is buttered on." It was important to remind Pavel of his past transgression just in case he forgot about it.

One day, you'll die, thought Pavel, *and I won't cry one salty tear.*

Rosti didn't know who the buyer was but in time, he would find out, and he wasn't beyond using blackmailing tactics later on if it meant he could re-sell it for a higher price. Though he'd received his fee and protected the middleman, there were no guarantees about protecting the actual buyer.

Jerry's PR maven was going to be all over it, splashing it on social media...even though it had nothing to do with Jerry's career, his upcoming performances, or anything that would even remotely help grow the brand.

Collectively, Jerry's team shook their heads at this "impulse buy." Rozina tried to get it through Jerry's thick skull; he was now almost out of cash. He'd been told almost once a week by his team: there was no money to play around with. None! His accountant

Cathy Ann often whined to Rozina and implored her to watch how he spent his money. "I am not in charge of that man, Cathy Ann. So don't be pointing fingers," she said. "I don't mean to get pissy with you but I didn't tell him to buy this record, I didn't encourage him and I sure as shit didn't make any of the connections for him. That's all on Jerry."

But she did try to talk to him.

"You tell that Cathy Ann to get off my back, Roz!" Jerry screamed into the phone one morning at 3 a.m. when yoga and edibles (a very rare indulgence) weren't helping him sleep. His notorious insomnia meant he had free reign to bother any of his employees any time of day or night. Rozina put up with it because she was highly (extraordinarily, in fact) compensated, but her life was not her own. She and her husband lived a contained life on Argyll Road in the Ditmas Park section of Brooklyn, a lush, tree-lined section that was only blocks away from the hub of commerce along Flatbush Avenue. Take that all the way down to one end of the borough and you were at the Brooklyn Bridge; take it to the other, and you were close to Manhattan Beach, where Jerry and his misery lived.

Rozina and Eric had plans to retire to Florida, into the perpetual sunshine with other like-minded people in their age and income bracket. Eric had retired almost two years earlier from being a purchasing director in manufacturing. Once Rozina finally retired (and this was a big bone of contention between the couple), their grown kids would have to decide if they were going to move too or stay in New York. Their son was a dentist and lived in the Lower East Side, and their daughter was a professor who had purchased a farm in Upstate New York for the apple-picking and college vibe.

Rozina had now hit thirty-two years working with Jerry. Eric's main goal was to cajole Rozina into giving her notice and formally retiring within the year. She reluctantly agreed with the plan; she longed to be away from the New York winters, but she had her kids relatively nearby, and she was making an incredible salary working for Jerry that would be hard to leave behind.

The Florida Panhandle sounded exactly right. For some reason, she dreaded (no, something stronger: was paralyzed by) the thought that one day, she'd have to tell Jerry it was time for her to move on. But it wasn't quite the right time yet.

Jerry had gotten married in his early 20s, but the relationship soured after three years when his wife found out he couldn't keep his hands off the young female talent. One could only look the other way for so long, and sheepish apologies just didn't cut it anymore. Goldie didn't hold a grudge; what was the point? Fight for what was already done and over with? She moved to Israel to live near the beaches of Tel Aviv. Now she was doing her share of ogling the beautiful younger bodies. They kept in touch, but he never saw her again, although technically, they remained married.

His one true love, though, was never meant to be. The times had no tolerance for such a love affair and he didn't want to put her through the struggle that would most assuredly come their way. Every decade or so, he'd look back and regret that he didn't even try, then console himself by arguing that it wouldn't be much easier today with race relations the way they were.

It was 1965. Coltrane played The Half Note in New York, bassist Charles Mingus played at the Village Gate, and Hy Lobenfeld was building a band of the best and brightest. He was most famous not for the music his band played but for his legendary audition sessions that brought musicians from all over the country. He had an inscrutable poker face, so you never knew if he liked what he heard or if he hated it. It was only after the six-hour marathons that he announced his picks.

Frannie Milton was a musical genius who had stunned the jazz world with her impeccably beautiful playing on the tenor sax. How she didn't win the first tenor (or any tenor) seat in Hy's band was both a crime and a crying shame.

Jerry knew she deserved the spot. Even back then, barely a serious musician, he knew two things: he would always love her, and she would always have to fight tooth and nail to get the same chances that fell into his lap nearly every day of his life. Stew Goldmann was vicious in his quest to get the chair position. A boyhood friend of Jerry's, he had a behind-doors hissy fit with Hy and put Frannie down every way he could, even making things up about her to prove he was the more deserving. Sure enough, Hy placed Stew as the lead tenor. It was beyond laughable. All the other musicians knew she was the superior player.

By 3 a.m., all the selections had been made. The musicians called it a night, even though it was near dawn. The showdown had exhausted the piss out of everybody. Zombified, they stumbled out to the street to walk home if they lived nearby or to go grab taxis.

Jerry was one of the lucky ones. He'd fought hard and got a spot with the other tenors, led of course by Stew. When he found that out, he knew it only meant one thing: Frannie got a big fat zero.

As he headed down the corridor to drag himself up the stairs and outside, he saw Frannie with her back against the wall, head in her hands, sobbing. The tenderness in his heart took over.

"Frannie..."

"Yes, my love. How did you know I didn't make it." It wasn't a question; it was a statement of resigned defeat. Due to the grueling audition process, she had no more grace to accept failure. Tears tumbled down her cheeks.

"You know that seat has your name on it. They're just too chicken to let a girl in the band." He laughed at "girl." She was all woman.

"You know what I mean," Jerry added.

"I sure do. I'm too female and too chocolate for these old hacks. They wouldn't know creativity if it bit them in the balls."

Jerry reached out for her hand and she took it. There had never been anything romantic between them. This might not be the moment for such a thing, anyway.

"Come over to my place. It's in Queens. You can sleep in the cab ride over."

She peered up and smiled. "Um, you're married."

"She's at her sister's in Long Island and packing for Israel at this very moment. And anyway, we're done. Have been for years. Married on paper only."

Silence.

"I promise, my hand to God. I won't touch you. I'll sleep on the couch."

Frannie laughed. "How did you know I didn't want to be alone?"

"Just an educated guess. Come, it's comfy and quiet and you can sleep as late as milady wants. I won't bother ya."

Tongues would be wagging but Jerry didn't care. Frannie was a friend, a colleague, a trusted confidant. She'd gotten the short shrift so many times in her young career. It couldn't be easy for her to keep coming back for more abuse.

"I like the TV on to fall asleep to. Just not the news."

"Whatever you wish."

She fell asleep instantly once the cab took off for Queens. Jerry looked at the way her hair framed her face like a cloud. Her lips were always about to form a smile, even when she was sleeping. She kept her sax case between her feet on the floor. A pro through and through.

He guided her into his small one-family house and showed her the main bedroom, stopping in to get his pajamas and his night cream.

"No funny business, Mr. Z."

"Scout's honor. Sweet dreams. And if you want to talk, wake me up."

The moment her head found the pillow, she started snoring.

Who in the world would be drawn to this smarmy, sequined showman?

MAWs.

Middle-aged women.

They came in droves from Canarsie, Brighton Beach, Marine Park, from Red Hook and Sheepshead Bay and Gerritsen Beach. But not just from Brooklyn. They traveled from over the water in Bayonne and Hoboken, Montclair and Westfield and other towns in New Jersey. Driven by their husbands or (if widowed) carpooling it and using limos and car services, the bejeweled beauties came en masse with their tickets, some bought a year ago when this performance was first announced, and stuffed them into their brassieres to see this god of gyration, this sultan of schlock.

Jerry had everyone believing he was from the original St. Petersburg, born of his ancestors' struggles in the shtetls of Lvov. He checked all the boxes. He was brash and flirtatious and knew how to work a crowd, at least when he started out.

But career fatigue was beginning to show.

Jerry wasn't always such a pain in the *zhopa*. Rozina remembered a time when he was playful, joyful even, and couldn't wait to get up on stage. That was when his backup band was its happiest, too. There was a full contingent of other saxes (Jerry let them solo on occasion, something he would never consider later in his career), trumpets, trombones, drums from Africa and South America, cymbals, a timpani, and the whole range of strings from violin to viola to cello plus a famous bassist who "converted" from straight-ahead to smooth, subjecting him to much derision from his ex-colleagues). Once, for about half a year, Jerry also had a piccolo player and a klezmer clarinetist in his band.

Those were the days, she thought. He composed a lot of new music then and was open to touring Europe, of course, but also South Africa, the UAB, Scandinavia.... Yet the older he got, the more he developed a kind of allergy to going on the road. It was more of an agoraphobic response. The horizontal sameness of air travel spiked his anxiety. He preferred congested cities on the mainland. More people to reach in a smaller radius, and then he could hop home and shut the world out.

They did go to Oslo once and Rozina would never forget it. He refused to run through any of his songs with his band, so they worked on the music without him. She was required to go on the trip, which she loved the idea of, except that she was newly married and didn't want to be away from Eric. But being so wet behind the ears and working for an occasional tyrant, she didn't want to stir the pot, so she went. She immediately realized the wisdom of her decision. Never had she been out of the Tristate area, and the frosty countryside far away from New York was breathtaking, the people lovely and welcoming. They were there for ten days, and at the beginning, Jerry took her around to the different sights and restaurants along with his security staff and his manager Frankus Taylor. After a week of sold-out performances and manic schedules, Rozina was exhausted. On their last day before flying back to the US, Jerry wanted to try out a few new songs and asked everybody to be available to run through them. At two in the afternoon, they went to the studio and waited. And waited. By four o'clock, with his final show only hours away, he was nowhere to be found.

Rozina was getting worried and texted him several times. Finally, a text came back.

I'm in a barn about 25 mi away

Rozina's jaw dropped. *What are you doing there? They're all here to work the new material.*

I'm getting anxiety treatments. Dont forget I took my therapist and aroma person along.

Jerry—

She steeled herself and took a moment.

The band needs you for some input.

Chrissakes! The "new" stuff is from last year. Not really new at all!

He was wrong, of course, but he responded: *The playlist is rote. They know what to do. If not, I'll fire them when we get back home.*

And so it went. Rozina refused to allow it to ruin the mood. She sat in on the rehearsal and they sounded excellent. Fabulous, even. And Jerry was a ghost.

Maybe he'd choke on his lavender and myrrh and they could end the tour without him. There wasn't a soul in the room who'd be sad about it.

Rozina kept insisting to her husband Eric that Jerry had never done anything inappropriate. He was just a douche, plain and simple.

“He has a child’s view of the world, very immature,” she told him when they were on their patio, gathering whatever warmth was available from the November sun. “I don’t know if he acts that way on purpose. That’s why I cut him some slack.”

“Well, still, he gives you a hard time. He has you go with him on tour when it’s not really necessary. That time he reamed you out at the rehearsal last year? There was no excuse for how he yelled at you and embarrassed you in front of the band.”

Rozina rubbed at her wrist. She did it whenever she felt the need to self-soothe.

“Well, yeah, it was pretty awful.” Her wrist was turning red. She pulled out her sleeve to cover it up and cupped her hands around her decaf. “I don’t think I told you this part. After the set was over, I wheedled my way onto the stage to talk to him privately for a few minutes before we went to get ready for dinner.”

“This was in San Fran, right?”

“Yup. He was wiping off his sax and shaking the spit out of it. The audience was getting up. Some people went to the back exits, and a few of them came milling over to the stage. They had dimmed the lights onstage and—they do this—they put up a chair barrier to discourage people from coming up to try to talk with the band. Just one of his antisocial quirks.”

"One of many, huh."

"Mmm-hmm. They redirected the rest of the fans to leave. Now it was just us onstage. So I stood there and looked dead at him. He was holding his favorite sax that he calls Violet. Don't ask. I've been with him so long that I know it by the sound of it."

She sipped from her cup. Decaf *and* no flavor. What was the point?

"He kind of smiled, but then he backed up and said, 'Okay Rozzie, what is it? Don't get to close to my baby, now.'"

She shook her head at the memory.

"At first, I just glared at him. The curtains came down in front of us and there was no chance of anybody hearing our conversation, so I lit into him. I let a few expletives fly. I didn't tell you this part?"

"First time hearing it," Eric answered. "I sure hope you kneed him in the groin. Go on."

"I should have, believe me. He's a man-child who needs a nanny. I mean, it's because of him that we live like this—" she gestured around her. Their Argyll Road neighborhood was one of the prettiest in Brooklyn and their house was a lovely Victorian on a cul-de-sac. Extraordinarily rare for such a gentrified part of the city. "But he's really a simpleton. A complainer, obsessed with his image, his brand, his, uh, masculinity, if you could even call it that. Screaming at me was beyond the limits of acceptable. And he's done it before, with everybody from his manager to that poor old accountant of his, Cathy, even his Israeli bodyguard. They ignore him, but I just couldn't let him get away with it."

"He knows your value as his admin. How stupid to have a meltdown like that."

She pulled her jacket around her. Almost time to give up on the paltry sun. "I gave it to him. I told him if he ever, *ever* spoke to me like that again, he'd be out on his ass without me. Him and Violet."

"What was he mad about in the first place?"

"We were in the studio that morning and his drummer had missed a whole section in the intro of one of his songs. He went back to his office and the phone in the studio rang. When I went to tell him his doctor was on the phone, he just flipped out on me. He was really mad at the drummer but I got the brunt of it. I was furious at him the rest of the day and held my tongue until after the show."

"Glad you set him straight, hun. I love my baby when she's feisty." Eric put his hand on her shoulder and squeezed gently. "It is getting chilly, I'll grant you that."

She had almost quit that night. And now, after three-plus decades under her belt and with Eric always hinting that she should retire, she was thinking about it again.

She deserved a second act. The question was, would Jerry give her up without a fight?

The venue was way too small and Jerry didn't want to accept the gig. But his manager insisted that Delaware Water Gap in Pennsylvania was a "sizzling hotbed of jazz" and he'd be foolish to turn away from the potential ticket sales.

"But Frankus, the damned *Poconos*? Come on. People soak in heart-shaped bathtubs there and they think it's romantic. It reminds me of the deserted Catskills: years past its prime. A has-been place. I'm no has-been!" Jerry whined.

"There's a long tradition of live jazz with a three-day festival on Labor Day weekend. It's the quiet little Woodstock of jazz. Plus, I got nothing else for you right now. Go play it."

Rozina did her research and, as usual, printed out her location analysis. It wasn't shabby. The site was adjacent to a university town with a thriving music program and several community bands.

Also in her report were the stats on the growing influx of New Yorkers since 9-11. They traveled in a straight shot, an hour and a half west on the interstate. For culture-seekers in neighboring New Jersey, it was an even shorter drive. They were all seeking the quaint B&B action and looking for outcrops of culture, of which Jerry considered himself a part. Jerry would provide a night of jazz with the beautiful Shawnee Mountains surrounding them.

Because Jerry didn't like to go on the road without some muscle, he took Kerim Mizrahi, a former Mossad agent who'd been with him since he moved to Manhattan Beach. Jerry had stolen him from the biggest venue in Chicago, putting an offer on the table that he couldn't turn down. He paid for Kerim to relo to Brooklyn and now the bodyguard called Park Slope, Brooklyn, his home. It was across the borough from Jerry's palatial estate, but Kerim already had his connections in the community. He knew the head of security at the hospital in the Slope and could use the helipad in an emergency.

Kerim picked up an added responsibility when Jerry started getting threatening notes at concerts with, of all things, a delivery of a bouquet of flowers. They were roses and, very oddly, a matte black color. Not airbrushed—grown that way. Rozina was terrified and told her husband, who was, among other things, an avid gardener and knew a little about cross-pollinating seeds and modifying plants. "I'm sure it's a spurned lover or something," he told her, trying to calm her down. "And since you're not actually at most of his concerts, I wouldn't worry. Unless they start sending flowers to his office. Then maybe he needs to have Kerim there 24-7."

When Jerry saw Rozina's reaction the first time black flowers landed in his dressing room, he came up with a plan. The next day, he put Frankus on speaker and called Kerim into the room. Rozina was already there, taking notes.

"Frankus, I told you I got a disturbing delivery at the Connecticut casino, right?"

"You did. Just tell me again. I want to see if we need to alert the police."

Kerim bristled. He didn't like Frankus calling the shots here. This was a security issue.

"Okay, so after the show, I went into my dressing room. By the way, the cleaning staff was just finishing up, and as I was going in, this guy in a work uniform came in wheeling a garbage can. I assumed he was about to empty my trash."

Kerim and Rozina exchanged glances.

"No!" Jerry clapped for emphasis. "I know what you two are thinking. Don't implicate a poor schlep who is just doing his job. It couldn't have been him because...because he's a working man. Impossible! I reject that out of hand."

Jerry had had his say.

"I rule nothing out at this point," Kerim said.

Frankus waited a beat before responding. "Please continue," he offered.

"Okay. As I told you, the note, which I hold in my hand now, reads: 'Dear Hack, Go Back, To Russia with Love, since that's where you belong, certainly not doing a song.'"

Though this was very serious, Rozina stifled a laugh by biting down hard on her right cheek.

"Did you notify the police?" Frankus asked.

"About the bad poetry?"

Rozina could just picture the look on Frankus's face. He didn't suffer fools gladly, which meant he would not tolerate any nonsense from Jerry.

"No, JERRY. About the threat."

“No. I did not. I don’t see a direct threat.”

“Well, you brought Kerim on the call. Hello, Kerim, by the way.”

“Hallo, sir.” About time he was acknowledged.

They came up with a costly solution, which they all admitted could work. But only if Jerry agreed to notify the police if this kind of thing ever happened again.

The plan was to identify all the florists in the area prior to every performance and pay them to shut down completely for two full days, the day before a performance and the day of, and to be on the alert in case any black roses had been ordered. This would even work for online orders, as it was the local florists who ultimately had to fill the jobs. This little workaround would cost Jerry in the neighborhood of two grand a day for each shop, so easily between ten and twenty thousand dollars for suburban areas and up to twice that for big cities. Cathy Ann, his accountant, blanched when she heard about it, but it bought Jerry peace of mind, and it was the only way he’d agree to go on tour.

Although it qualified as being a "hole in the wall," the restaurant/bar in the Pocono Mountains wasn't to be sneezed at. The crowd joggled their feet along to the music and there was an occasional outburst of "Yes!" Hokey honeymoon resorts and potholed roads notwithstanding, the door receipts were fairly healthy. After two encores and a few exaggerated bows, it was time to shuffle backstage and get changed. Jerry stepped over the flowers that had been tossed on stage (sadly, no more thongs; a sign of inevitable decline), thrust his sax at a set assistant and wound his way to his dressing room.

His jumpsuit was made of micro-thin Gore-Tex (ten percent rayon) and was supposed to wick the sweat from his body; it seemed to do the exact opposite. Slamming the door behind him, he regarded himself in the circular surround of mirrors.

Bloated red face. Zippers straining to hold in his sausage thighs. Threadbare fabric beneath the armpits. It was time to dump this outfit and start using his backup. Rozina would need to order another dozen, if his career held out that long. If he held out that long.

Then he saw them. A bunch of black roses in a tall vase. This one was bigger than previous vases, with a square bottom that swirled upward. The etched vines in the glass told him this wasn't a dime-store purchase. *Ahh, my biggest fan. Come out, come out, whoever you are.* He leaned in to smell the flowers and was hit with their powerful fragrance. He lifted the vase and saw a number ten envelope under it. *What will it say this time? Break a leg? Break my neck? Retire already?*

This was getting ridiculous. The security detail here was a joke. All they cared about was their take. Hadn't Rozina instructed management to watch for anything unusual? Surely a huge bouquet of black flowers said something weird was afoot.

And why was he playing for peanuts? That was another question. Adding in all the liquored-up patrons, the house made a killing; his take was smaller than warranted for this market, which was basically an extension of New York and New Jersey. It made him angry just thinking about the money. He chomped down and shook his head vigorously.

In order to have placed the flowers on the table in his dressing room, somebody had to personally bring them in without being seen, but who? His own staff or the club's?

There was one bright spot: the flowers were still alive. Last time, the mystery person delivered two dozen dead flowers, and that prompted a swift call to the cops. Yet nothing was done. That was the evening Rozina swore off working the events. She wasn't required to be at any of his shows, but he paid her extra to come and eavesdrop on the audience members. He expected her to report back what was being said about him.

Out of curiosity, Jerry opened the envelope. This guy was funny. Or maybe it was a woman. Sick, but funny.

"Four (Reasons Why)"

There are four
Reasons why
That I think you're a hack
And I'll start-

Four
Reasons why
You just suck at the sax. I'll
impart:

One,
You have no sense of
timing You sure can't
swing

Two
Is disregard for melody You
butcher that thing.

Hey, there are four Reasons
why
You should never
Have made it
To fame

Three
Would be your boring solos
Putting us to sleep

Four
And this is worst of all

Your vibe ain't deep

There are four reasons why
You should just give up jazz
And I've named them

Maybe
Your fans
Laugh at you
'Cuz you know you've shamed them!

Paying off the florists clearly wasn't working. There had to be another solution to this because God knew the venue owners didn't have a clue. Why hadn't his own head of security been able to prevent it from happening?

Frankus Taylor was tasked with connecting Jerry Zolotov with a famous framer who made highly sought-after, custom-designed art frames for the rich and insecure. Jerry's bone record needed to have the perfect context. It was Frankus's job to then get Jerry's promotions team (at the moment, a "team" of one, David Migliori) to "leak" it to the press.

Through his connections in the art world, Frankus identified three contenders who came with spotless recommendations. He was waiting for Jerry to reject them, but his boss was uncharacteristically pleased with all three. Ultimately, Jerry chose an artist whose debut pieces were shepherded immediately to the top galleries in New York, San Francisco and Chicago, followed by a tour to Paris, Milan and London.

The commission went to an artist from Wyoming who was a jazz lover, and though she was not into Jerry's style, could speak intelligently on music. It was her similar interest in bone records and her own connection to Russia (her mother had immigrated to the US in 1946, when she was an infant, at a time when flights to the States were still permitted) that piqued Jerry's interest. What sealed the deal was her use of gold foil and abstract design that evoked flow and movement.

Her fee was seven thousand dollars, which included the wood of the southern California jacaranda tree for the frame, the archival quality matte, special UV and sound-protective glass, and the gold foil. Jerry asked her how long it would take to finish, and she told him two months.

"Get to it," he muttered. Then he softened it with, "Thank you. I'm sure it will be beautiful."

She'd dealt with other socially awkward clients before, but she never had to sign an NDA like this one. Jerry had his attorney include language that prohibited her from taking about or disseminating photos of the artifact until the project was complete. Then after it was finished and paid for, she was allowed to show her work but had to blur out half of the record. If she agreed to post a picture of it with a link to any of Jerry's CDs, he would allow her to show a photo of the whole piece to immediate family members, but only by showing them her phone, not sending it in a text or email. After a deep, silent sigh, she signed the NDA and got to work.

A stunning view of the Atlantic was the reason Jerry bought his house in Manhattan Beach. Most of the rooms faced the water. His office had vaulted ceilings and windows from the floor up. The daytime light was spectacular; the nighttime view of the stars looking down on the white-tipped waves was just as breathtaking. It was here, in his office—not his many lounges or his plush theater—that he did his best thinking, whether he was planning a playlist or throwing a mental dart at the map to figure out where he was going to tour next.

There was no question where the bone record was going to be hung. Behind his ultra-ergonomic smart office chair (that had a heater for the tush and cushions designed to fit his every lump and bump) was a pale coral wall that the masterpiece would call home.

Two months dragged along. When he received the heavily insured package, he was, for once in his life, speechless. Genuine tears sprang from his eyes. What had started as an act of ego and arrogance and "I'll show them"—whoever *them* was—was now symbolic of his having arrived, of earning what he had only dreamed was possible in his down-and-out days.

"Tell that girl from Wyoming she did a bang-up job. Nobody has anything like this," Jerry gushed to Rozina. She was working from home, taking a rare three days off to sleep in with Eric and have dinner at a new place each day.

"Well, congratulations, you finally got yourself a bone record," Rozina said unemphatically. "Just think. You're the only person on the planet who has such a rare record in a custom-made piece of art."

"I know. I'm blessed." It was a simple statement said quietly.

That made her feel bad for being such a cynic.

"Did you have Kerim over to see it yet?" she asked in a lighter tone.

"He's on his way now. There was an accident on the Belt Parkway, and he had to take the streets. I love my Israeli. Don't you?"

"Better be sure all your sensors are in place," she responded. "Once your press release goes out, there's no telling who's going to drop over for a visit."

"When are you coming over to see it?"

"Thursday. I'll tell Migliori to get on it immediately. Now that you have it safe and sound, I want to be sure he writes this up nicely and gets it into TMZ and Huff, the New York and the London Times—I mean, why not?—and all that good PR stuff."

"Thanks, Roz. Tell Eric I said hi."

"Will do."

Nobody was prepared for the amount of trouble that this new showpiece was going to cause, least of all Jerry Z.

♪

It wasn't any of Kerim's business what expensive hobbies Jerry entertained or how he spent his money. But as someone who came from poverty, Kerim was stunned the first time he walked into Jerry's office and saw the bone record hanging on the wall.

"You like?" Jerry was filing his nails and had his feet up on his gargantuan walnut desk. The housekeeper had recently polished it and the place smelled of varnish.

"Well, yes, I know that." Kerim produced a tight smile. "We wired it up to the security system, remember?"

As Jerry launched into its history, Kerim relaxed. A happy boss was an agreeable boss, one who didn't send his employees out on any weird security details, like the time he ordered Kerim to inspect the kitchens of all his favorite restaurants in Sheepshead Bay and Little Odessa, looking for arsenic and other ingredients that shouldn't be there. It was a particularly paranoid period that Kerim would rather forget.

"So what do you think? I paid quite a lot of shekels for that."

Kerim winced. Even though Jerry was Jewish (quietly), somehow his use of the word seemed belittling.

"Well, Jerry, you work hard, so why not play hard."

"But you didn't ask *by how much* I play hard."

"I know from this discussion that it's quite valuable to you and that you paid a huge sum."

Why isn't he giving me the satisfaction of telling him what I paid? Jerry's skin prickled.

"Over two million dollars. Two point seven. So you see, it's an important thing for my head of security to know, yes?"

The varnish was overpowering. Jerry really needed a better exhaust system. *Maybe the vents are clogged,* Kerim mused. He'd have to talk to housekeeping in the morning.

"Like I said, it's obviously very important to you. The dollar amount? Impressive but secondary."

"Ha!" Jerry nearly screamed. He put down his nail file. "Not secondary if you ask Frankus Taylor. That jerkface."

"He's just looking out for you. Like we all are."

Kerim sighed. Jerry was the most insecure person he'd ever met. He had a lot of fans and admirers and had attained a level of success most people only dreamed about. There was no filling that empty space, but sometimes expensive baubles helped cover it up.

A boxy, midnight blue sedan slowly came into view on the monitor at eleven p.m. on a Tuesday. Kerim was staying at Jerry's home for the weeks following the bone record installation in case of something exactly like this. He was given special instructions to be extra vigilant for chatter the moment Jerry purchased the bone record. Now that his prized possession was inside the house, Jerry was sure word would get out, and he wasn't wrong.

Kerim carefully slipped his Jericho 9mm inside his waistband. He went straight to the Mossad for his weaponry. It was extremely advanced. Kerim wasn't fooling around.

He came out a side door in a heavily hedged section of the grounds and watched. The vehicle had no rear plates, no decals, no stickers. He was about to aim a new device (the latest technology) that could read a VIN number from thirty feet away when the car revved hard and sped off. Interestingly, the tire tracks were nearly nonexistent. All that was visible was a mash-up of patterns. Maybe the guy (he assumed) had a set of custom-made combo treads to escape identification. They had those in Israel. He'd have to look into it.

Kerim waited a few minutes in silence, then slowly walked the perimeter of the grounds. Nobody, nothing. Just the sound of the ocean's nocturnal breath.

Jerry was sound asleep, and Kerim didn't think the situation warranted waking him up. In the morning, he'd tell Jerry what he saw and they'd watch the security tape again. Decisions would have to be made about reporting it to the authorities.

The Stalin baby X-ray record was none the wiser. It wouldn't be the only attempt on its life, though.

Jerry was sleeping in later and later these days. His next performance wasn't for two more months when he'd hit the Carolinas, DC, Florida and back up to Missouri and Oklahoma.

The ocean breeze was not a motivator to get out of bed, but he heard the clanking of coffee cups from the kitchen. Coffee sounded like a great reason.

He went to pee and stared straight ahead at a man in the mirror that he didn't recognize. His hair was frizzy, spotty, a mousy shade of brown mixed with dull gray. Nothing near the slick salt-and-pepper look he paid his stylist for. His eyebrows were an unattractive tangle, yet the stubble on his upper lip and chin had slowed to near-nothingness. He lamented the inability to grow facial hair anymore. He used to be a sexy devil.

His urine stream was erratic. He looked down at his anatomy and shook his head. It had been a long time since he'd actually used it. The fan mail had died down, and nobody was showing up naked in his dressing room anymore.

He washed up and swished his mouth with some blue rinse. "You used to be handsome. What in the holy hell happened to you?"

Kerim had made coffee, a dark and intense blend from the Sheepshead Bay farmer's market.

"What else did you get there?" Jerry asked.

"Oh, you know. Those cranberry vanilla scones you enjoy. Some toffee chocolate for me. And a few crusty loaves of bread. I know you love those."

"I'm turning into a crusty loaf myself," Jerry said, spreading his fingers over his paunch.

"So, J. Something I need to share. You ready to hear it?" Kerim knew he needed to prep Jerry for even the smallest bit of bad news. The dark blue vehicle—well, there was no way to sugarcoat that.

"Yes, thank you for asking. Then again, it's what I pay you for. Mightily, I will add."

A small smile came to Kerim's face and quickly faded. "Last night at 11:06 p.m., this car slid into the right side of the driveway." He tilted his phone so Jerry could see.

"It remained there for four or five minutes, then he rolled away," he added.

"Plates?"

"Regrettably, none. Also, the tires are Frankensteins, so there's no IDing the model."

"What do you mean?" Jerry asked.

"Apparently, some kind of off-market hybrid tires that leave special tracks to confuse law enforcement. I have to look into that."

A crumb fell onto Jerry's shirt. He pulled up his shirt and sucked in the little piece of food.

"Okay, what about the VIN?"

"Nothing. The app didn't pick it up. Maybe the car was scrubbed."

"Goddamn it!"

"I put this into the log. I can run a report on blue sedans, but, you know."

"Not worth the pile of dogshit info you'll get. Let's just keep a watch. Did you have the security triangulated around my office? Make sure it's wired up in case of a break-in. I mean, God forbid." The vanilla scone was the right choice.

"Yes, we've already done that."

It didn't seem Jerry understood what measures had been put in place.

"Look, I went to great expense to get this record," Jerry added.

Kerim nodded dramatically. "I got it."

"I know you do. I'm just reiterating. I insured it for a crapload, and you're here with me, always ready for action. So I'm not going to go crazy with worry. This guy, girl, whoever. Keep an eye out."

Sometimes Kerim thought he could just walk away from all of this and get his own beach house. He tossed back his tight black curls and finger-combed his bangs. He could still catch a handball game at the Coney Island boardwalk. "You want I should stay?"

"Ahh. I see that faraway look in your eyes. Time to watch those beautiful young ladies speed-walking on the boardwalk. Anyway, I have things to do."

Kerim smiled. He needed some romantic release soon, or he was going to snap.

"Your backup should be here any second, right? I say go enjoy the day. I gotta get my stylist in here and take care of this mess on top of my head."

"Okay-dokay, boss man."

The Israeli took his leave and texted his subordinate, a retired New York City cop with a cranky disposition.

Jerry went into his office and looked lovingly at the bone record and at the exquisite frame it was in. He decided to fire up his computer to research the top collectors and see if any of them had police records. Maybe he could find out what they drove.

One name that kept cropping up was his cousin Pavel from Ukraine. But he wasn't even in the US. And anyway, Jerry thought, why would he go after something that he told Jerry about in the first place, and had been paid very well for?

♪

"The florists. Did you pay them?" The booming voice came from the bathroom.

As always, Rozina was two steps ahead of Jerry. That was job security; as long as she could anticipate his neurotic needs, he'd find her of value to "the team." Only now, thoughts of an exit sign took up most of her time.

"I did. There are only three within a five-mile radius and—"

"Well! What about further out? I do *not* want a replay of the Poconos debacle!" he yelled out.

She tried not to sound smug as she yelled back, "And if you didn't cut me off, yes, I went all the way to look for florists from central Jersey, in case they're driving over the bridge, to fifty miles all around here. Wilkes-Barre, the Lehigh Valley, up to Philadelphia."

"Okay, no geography lesson needed." He chuckled to himself. Philly was a great market. *I need to go back there. Philly loves smooth jazz.*

Opening for New Age icon Vanji was a big deal. Although he shouldn't be the opener at this point in his career, Vanji was a billionaire, so maybe a little of that luck would rub off on him.

Rozina heard the toilet flush. She winced.

He came back into his office, waving his hands to air them dry. *Thank God,* Rozina thought.

"So tell me about the City of Brotherly Love. Kerim is on board with everything? He knows the lay of the land, so to say? No flowers there to greet me, right? It's only two weeks away."

"Yup. He's thoroughly up to date. Not a corner left unexplored. He even has Uber, Lyft and the little local concierge services on notice."

Jerry flumped into his ergonomic executive chair. He wanted to run through a few songs. The audience always loved when he did his improv and played with the main theme, sometimes incorporating other (more popular) songs in the smooth jazz catalog. His first platinum single, "Green Grass at Sunrise," was such a runaway hit he could play that for ninety minutes and nobody would mind.

"Get the studio ready at eleven. Please." He gave her a boyish smile. "I want to work on a few new riffs. Gotta keep these audiences on their feet."

The only ones coming to their feet would be the ones who paid to see Vanji. New Age was hot again, but smooth jazz, not so much. It had its heyday briefly, shooting up in the charts on the heels of the R&B and blue-eyed soul of the '80s and right before New Age really took hold. It was jazz for the masses; you didn't have to be an intellectual to "get" smooth jazz. There was no requirement to notice key changes or complex rhythms or harmonies that teetered on dissonance like in traditional jazz.

In the hands of Jerry Zolotov, songs were accessible, listenable, easy to follow. Though his technique had faltered slightly through the years, his vibrato was as strong as ever. All the gimmicks worked every time. Hell, the crowds went wild when he just held a note for a long time and danced around like a baboon.

Jerry had a rock-hard shell around him. He was impervious to criticism, ridicule, and even mysterious black roses. "Smooth jazz" might be a lesser kind of music in the eyes of some purist beboppers, but Jerry knew that people saw smooth as an escape. It was fun, easy to hear, and, most of all, happy.

The Briggs School of Music had put him on staff for master classes which always filled up, and when he played the college circuit, students made fake tickets to get in to see him. This went on for years. When he played the festivals, day-long concerts and endless benefit events, there was always a huge, undulating sea of people dancing to his music.

In the late '90s, it was a different story. It was then that the taunts started coming. The critics took aim with their pens, calling him a "faux talent," "an artificial vibemeister" and "a musician who dials it in for the yawning masses."

The mocking anonymous letters that had recently been mysteriously delivered to his dressing room broke the camel's back. He pretended to laugh and gave the blackened roses to his staff or just threw them in the garbage. The letters, he kept. *If there's anything fishy going on,* he thought, *I have something to show the police.* He didn't know how serious they were or if they were a threat to his safety, but you can never be too careful.

One evening in mid-December, while he was thinking about a holiday gig he had for a corporate party, he sat and stared at his sax. Of all the saxes he owned, including two sopranos, twelve altos, six tenors and three baritones, he favored a sturdy Japanese-made horn he named Violet. It had the sweetest sound of all. Way back in the 1920s, it had belonged to the principal saxophone player of the Viennese Limited Orchestra. He'd even heard a few recordings of theirs and swore he could pick out the sax.

"Violet, tell me. I know you will be honest."

He brushed aside the hate mail (pre-screened by Rozina) that had started to accumulate, then wiped the wetness from his eyes.

"Am I a hack?"

As he asked, he tenderly took the instrument from its deep velvet case and placed it on his lap. It hardly gleamed anymore, but it had something better: a patina. From being handled, played and loved.

He glanced outside. The clock read 1:45 a.m., and he just couldn't fall asleep. A steady rain was falling, but the forecast said it would clear up within the hour. Just enough time to do some woodshedding. He'd always wanted to play outdoors at one of New York City's iconic spaces like the world-famous tenor master Sonny Rollins.

"Nobody can call me a fake and get away with it!" he screamed to the ocean. "I will play for the people of New York and New Jersey at the same time. Then you tell ME who's a hack!"

With that, Jerry put on his jacket and tucked a mini umbrella into his back pocket. He was going to the

Verrazano Narrows Bridge to do what the greats had done before him. Play to the world.

And this time, he was going alone. Really alone. Without his chauffeur or Kerim, without bothering Rozina, which he realized he'd done enough of in her long career with him. She was starting to look a little frazzled, a little more her age. He made a mental note to take it easier on her from now on. If he was getting tired of the whole ball of wax, she was, too.

The drive wouldn't take too long from his home in Manhattan Beach. He'd be extra careful on the slick roads.

Jerry's SUV pulled out of its double-wide driveway, and Jerry pressed the button on his remote. As the custom-hewn iron gates opened, he waved goodbye to the security camera and grinned as he passed it. Kerim should be asleep, but there was an outside chance he was watching the feed from his home at the other end of Brooklyn.

I'll tell him I went woodshedding, but later. Because now, he'll only tell me not to go. Right, Violet?

One block turned into another until it yielded to the Belt Parkway. He knew where the pull-off was on the other side of the road, pointing back to Brooklyn. He'd have to head into Jersey, pay the toll, and then turn around so he could be facing Brooklyn again.

This happened with frequency during the day. At 2 a.m., not so much. There were no toll collectors, no cops, just E-ZPass, and of course everything was captured on cameras. "Love Me Tender" blurted out of his phone, which was Kerim's ringtone. *Crap!*

"Yes, I'm driving. I didn't go far. Why are you up?"

"Aren't you *glad* I'm up, Jerzy?"

"I guess. What is it? I'm trying to get in the right head to play to the world."

"But why are you in your car? Where are you going, Jerzy?"

Only a little bit more to the tolls.

"The Verrazano. And no, I'm not crazy."

Kerim's cortisol ticked up a notch. This was stupid and impulsive. "I see. You and Mr. Sonny Rollins. He was on the Williamsburg."

"The Verrazano has nicer views. The Palisades..."

"Jerry, are you seriously going out to play right now? It's nasty out. How long are you going to be there?"

This was exasperating. He didn't need a mommy. He knew how to drive in all kinds of weather.

"One hour. I promise. I know you're looking out for me."

"And you're alone?"

"Just me and Violet. I would have loved to bring that brunette gofer with the cute tush who worked the casino with us, but her boyfriend excels at martial arts. What can you do."

After a pause, Kerim said sleepily, "Text me when you're back home. Be careful."

"Roger that. Go back to bed with that honey who's there with you. Whoever she is."

"Mmft. Nite."

It was aggravating to be monitored constantly. Jerry sighed. *That's what I pay him for, I guess.* The blue necklace lights on the Verrazano brought his eye to the toll booths. He was almost at his turnaround point.

Suddenly, he felt giddy. He'd always wanted to do this. Maybe it was juvenile, something an insecure newbie does for validation. There was nobody here but the seagulls. As he went through and carefully maneuvered his U-turn at the tolls, he entered the

Brooklyn-bound side. Then he slowed to 25 mph so he wouldn't miss the pull-over spot.

All he had on was a thin Gor-Tex rain jacket over one of his old stage outfits, a gaudy jumpsuit that he was thinking of getting rid of anyway. If he was going to do this right, he might as well be stylish. Maybe he could take the jacket off long enough to snap a selfie. That would look great on Twitter.

There was no traffic to be seen. Then, something lucky: a sign that read *lane closed ahead.* That meant nobody would accidentally plow into him and he could park safely.

He was almost at a crawl when he saw the orange cones in front of him and pulled over. When the car came to a stop, he took a deep breath, then let it out in a huge huff.

Violet, my love. It's just you and me and the rain.

He opened the case and looked at the reflection of the bridge on the sax's body. How beautiful, he thought. Why did I wait so long to do this? As he assembled his instrument, he realized he only had one reed left. Too bad he didn't check first. He'd have to make this one last. It wasn't new, so hopefully there were no cracks in it. *Oh well, Violet, you'll just have to forgive me if I squeak.*

He looped the neck strap over his head, then turned around. There was still no traffic coming. He opened his door carefully and stepped out and immediately went around the front of his SUV, almost tripping on a cone. He clipped the sax to his neck strap and took the mouthpiece out of his pocket.

The railing was dripping as the rain turned up the volume. Maybe being here on the bridge wasn't the most brilliant idea, but he was here already. He'd run through a few fast tunes and call it mission accomplished.

Suddenly, a pair of headlights edged into his lane. For a moment, Jerry was terrified. Then he recognized the keyboard-shaped grille. Stew Goldmann. *How did he find out I'm here?*

"Jerry!" he called, pulling up the hood of his anorak. Jerry could see Stew's driver staring straight ahead through the vigorous wipers.

"What the hell, Stew! What are you doing here? It's two in the goddamn morning!"

"I know. I could ask the same question of you."

The men hugged, leaving space for the sax between them.

"Woodshedding? At this hour?" Stew asked his friend.

"Did Kerim tell you I was here? I'll have to read him the riot act tomorrow. What is he thinking, waking you up for this?"

Stew rubbed the rain from his face. "Ah, don't give him a hard time. He worries about you."

The son I never had, thought Jerry.

"Well, you gonna play or what? Hurry it up and let's get out of this rain."

Jerry shook his head. Tears formed in his bloodshot eyes, but they were washed away by the rain. He was getting colder and wetter with every passing minute, to say nothing of the personal embarrassment that had come over him.

"I'm here because I have something to prove. You know, they say I'm a hack." Jerry smirked. "I think they're right."

Stew looked down. In his younger days, he played the tenor, too. He was the lead in Hyman Rifkin's band. It didn't last long, though: less than a year later, he got hot-headed in a bar when an out-of-work bass player accused Stew of bullying his way to the top. In the fracas, Stew was on the receiving end of an incredibly strong punch and got his lip split open. His embouchure would never be the same. That was when he decided to get into music promotion. He wouldn't be caught dead using an electronic wind instrument; it just wasn't the same as wailing away on a saxophone.

"Jerry, stop. You're great. The audience loves you. You hit platinum three times in your career. It doesn't get much better than that."

"I have shtick and artifice," he scolded Stew. "You? My friend, you stand head and shoulders above all of us. Raw talent. Even if you had switched to electronic, it would be exactly the same. The world just wasn't ready for you. And why? Because of bloviating asshats like me jumping around on stage *saying look at me, look at me!*"

Jerry said what needed to be said and suddenly felt relieved. He was existentially exhausted from the charade. It was time to stop all the nonsense. Stew was really good. Not as good as Frannie, the love of his life, but Jerry had put that away in a little box, as he did

Stew's discrediting her to get into Hy Lobenfeld's band. That was forgiven many years ago.

"Okay, I'll admit it," his boyhood friend said. "You have the gimmick part down pat. But underneath that proud peacock stuff is a flawless technique, pacing that's as gorgeous as Bach and an uncanny knack for reading an audience and serving them what they really came for."

Jerry frowned. "Come on. I'm a phony-baloney. Plain and simple. I should really step down so the younger players can have a fair shot at it because God knows that Jerzy Zolotov is neurotic, narcissistic and couldn't hold down a tune if he sat on it."

Stew considered his friend's self-criticism and realized something must be going on, but what was it? Why was he losing his mojo now? Jerry was revered, beloved, the object of affection of fans all over the globe and on other planets too, if they had jazz. It didn't matter one tiny bit what the straight-ahead jazz world said about smooth. Fuck them.

Stew's burly driver came out with an umbrella the size of Montana and stood over both men. Jerry nodded his thanks but waved him off. Not only was he drenched, he was also numbed by the cold. He had underdressed. But the show must go on.

"Hey. We were both trained classically, J," Stew continued as he got back into his limo. "You studied opera and madrigals, and you took theory—then taught it—in all those university master classes. You play the shit out of everything you blow, and there's nobody like you. Why are you being so goddamned hard on yourself? You've packed the house for a lot of years and always got good reviews. Even the bad reviews have to admit how good you are."

"Maybe, but look at me now. I'm a puffed-up has-been, the sequins are poppin' off, and I have nothing new or real to contribute to the art form anymore."

I'm sick, he thought. *Sick of trying to prove to myself that I'm not a fraud. Maybe Goldmann will hear it now.*

"Hey, I'll show you what I mean. Just take a listen. I'll be quick, and then I'll get back in my car and we can just all go home."

Jerry shimmied the ligature onto the neck of his instrument and licked the reed with extra saliva so it would be pliant, then slipped on his custom-made gold and onyx mouthpiece ring to hold it in place.

The reed tasted funny. Maybe it was the salt spray coming up from the Narrows. And was his mouth getting numb? Must be the cold.

He placed his lips around the mouthpiece and inhaled extra deep to prepare for the first note, his signature high F sharp. Suddenly, his stomach clenched into an excruciating bolus of pain as he leaned over the railing. The aluminum platform under his designer sneakers was slippery and his right foot gave way, then his left. He was unable to pull back in time. Stew Goldmann watched in horror as in one quick movement his friend teetered forward and fell over the slick railing. There was no time to grab him. In a flash, amid a swirling helix of purple sequins, Jerry was gone, swallowed by the foamy black waters below.

Rozina had been walking around in shock ever since news broke of her boss's unexpected demise. Eric wouldn't bring up Jerry unless she did, exhibiting uncharacteristic restraint from instructing her how to deal with her emotions (something she often accused him of doing). After a week, he approached her gingerly. "How're you doing? Feel like talking?"

"Hon, please, let's do something new. How about a ride over to Neponsit? You know how you always say it's so clean and pretty in the winter? Not like these city beaches here. Or we can go deeper into the Island. What about going to Montauk Point for a week?"

She was on the ledge, almost ready to jump into life but at the same time, holding herself back, still processing what had happened. Nothing could be done about it, and it was time to get back to living life. Retirement had come at a cost, but she had no obligations now. It was time to exhale.

"I mean, I want to go. I really do," she said. "But I'm still feeling raw. Maybe I need therapy."

A light snow tinted the patio white. Eric swept a few crumbs off the dining room table and caught them in a napkin. Then he went to the sink and shook them out.

"Sure, why not, if it'll help you get through this. We can still have our getaway. These two things aren't mutually exclusive. I'll go look and see what it's like in Sag Harbor or Montauk this time of year. Same ocean, though. What about someplace warm?"

She hadn't even thought of that. Follow the sun.

Rozina didn't have to ask anybody's permission or play word games anymore. Jerry was gone, and she was a free bird. She was concerned about not getting paid out for her vacation time—her PTO bank showed twelve weeks—but Jerry's manager Frankus would make sure she got what she was owed with a little extra bonus. Rozina never knew it, but old Frankus had a thing for her all these years. He looked up at the ceiling and told Jerry he was paying her twice the customary bonus, and if Jerry had anything to say about it, he would need to come back to earth and fight it out.

Money didn't buy happiness, but it sure made things more comfortable for them. Eric was quietly supplementing his retirement with a hobby, and it was starting to take off: restoring and reselling war figurines online. It fit his studious and meticulous nature. He'd also made some pretty smart moves in the stock market. All things considered, this next phase of life for them would be a time to really let their hair down. They'd both worked very hard to get there.

"Do you think they'll ever find the killer?" Two vertical lines formed between Rozina's eyebrows.

"Probably at some point." He was almost finished painting a tin soldier from the early 1920s that he'd put up for sale. He even started to take on some of the kids' old toys, fixing them up and getting a small stream of cash from crafting and collectible sites.

"Do you think I need to be worried, I mean, about being questioned?"

Eric lifted the magnifiers from his eyes. “Why? Did you have it out for him?”

“I could almost say yes. He was difficult, definitely. But he paid me well, and sometimes I got some unexpected benefits. Our trip all over the Hawaiian islands, was that so terrible?”

“Not at all. Hey, come here.”

As Eric hugged his wife, something still didn’t sit right with her. Jerry would never get out of his car on a bridge. He was deathly afraid of heights. If his limo had to drive over a bridge or an overpass, he’d need to put on his earbuds and listen to some calming ambient noise. Rozina had ordered blackout eye masks that his driver kept in the glove box. Kerim kept a pair of them too, just in case the driver lost his.

“I can’t figure out why he was there that night. Stewie said that Jerry just wanted to ‘validate himself.’ Maybe he was having a hard time with something else that I didn’t know about.”

“Could be.” Eric looked into her wolf-gray eyes. “We all have stories we don’t tell, huh.”

“I’m not liking that little sound bite, Mr. Eric.” She smiled and accepted a kiss on the lips.

“Really, Rozina. You couldn’t have known all his demons or what drove him to jump. And if he didn’t jump, if he was pushed, who his enemies were. He got all those weird flower deliveries, right?”

“True. Well, I just hope they find him or her. Jerry had a lot of life left in him. He was planning on the jazz festivals in Scandinavia, and he seemed excited about touring again, like a little boy.”

“That little boy had some big goings-on. I remember you telling me about his parents being so hard on him, and there was a woman he fell in love with who he wasn’t supposed to be hanging around. And that ex-wife, who took off to Israel. Who knows? You can’t worry about it. Now, what tropical island should we plan on visiting? I’m ready to get out of this place.”

♪

Rozina fiddled with the hem of her Swiss dot skirt. She loved the boho look, it was so feminine. But lately, she wasn't feeling that way.

"What's up?" her therapist Sandy asked.

"I guess I'm still not myself with Jerry gone. What a horrible way to die."

"I could definitely understand that. It's terrifying."

"When I get up, I think 'what can I do to take my mind off things?' Then today, I thought wearing something pretty would pick up my mood."

"As if! I'd be changing clothes constantly."

"Yup. Flouncy, floozy, life's a doozy."

Sandy spit out her coffee. "Good one! Can I use it?"

"Sure. No charge."

"So how are you sleeping, Roz?"

Taking a sip of the mint green tea—Sandy always had different flavors to offer, and mint was refreshingly different—Rozina considered the question.

"I'm sleeping okay, but not Eric. He's tossing and turning. Last night, he was kicking around like he was running. He almost got me!"

"Wonder what's bothering him. Are you two okay?"

"I think so," she said quickly. There was no room for any marital issues. Life was stressful enough. And wasn't it time to start being present with each other, after all that had happened?

"I mean, he says he's really happy that I'm now officially an unemployed member of society. I mean, retired. I can't get used to saying that yet. And he's been planning lots of little getaways. I'm actually looking forward to them. He just better stop trying to kick me!"

"Maybe he's dreaming he's a squirrel being chased by a big dog."

Rozina laughed.

Sandy knew how fast fifty minutes flew by. Clients didn't usually realize the time they were eating into. "Let's talk about Jerry for a minute, if that's okay."

"Sure."

"No matter how this case turns out, you know you couldn't have prevented it, right?"

"I know. I mean, they'll get the person, I'm sure. If not the New York PD, then back in the USSR."

They smiled at the musical reference.

Sandy continued. "What was the last interaction you had with him?"

"I had to take his sax home with me because he had to fly out right after a performance and wanted to use another instrument. This was about a week earlier. By the way, he called it 'Violet.' Weird, right? Anyway, I drove it to his house—his palace, I should say—and he thanked me. Then he asked me if I wanted to come in to sit for a minute and talk. That was unusual."

"Interesting. Then what happened?"

"He told me that he was thinking of throwing in the towel. That he couldn't take all the black roses being sent—"

"That was a thing?"

"Oh. Well, I probably shouldn't have said that. But it's privileged information, just between us, right?"

"Yes. Unless you're the killer." Sandy gave a broad smile. "And we know you are not."

"Correct."

"So how did it make you feel, that he wanted to quit his career?"

The Swiss dots provided a pleasing texture, and she read the fabric like Braille. "At first, very sad. He was worn out about it. Just totally empty. He said there was nothing more he could give. I felt like he was being honest with me."

Sandra could see the creases on Rozina's chin and around her mouth. This was painful for her to recall.

When the muted chimes went off, Rozina stood and let out a deep breath. "I guess I need more time to process this and grieve. How long do you think it'll take? Eric wants to go-go-go."

Sandra looked at her with warm brown eyes and a calm smile. "When you're ready, if ever. You might put this in a little box and take it out when you feel sad. And you'll think about the good things you experienced with your boss. Your friend."

"I guess in a way he really was."

"Give your husband a little more credit. He just wants to see you happy."

"I suppose. Maybe he's grieving in his own way, for his own reasons."

"Could be. See you next week."

Picture any over-the-top, pathologically needy celebrity and you wouldn't even come close to Jerry Zolotov in his final years.

For his last concert (and, had he known it was his last, he would have amped it up some more), he wore a skin-tight, shark tooth-patterned royal blue suit with knotted fringes. His screaming bleached-white hair was teased into a frizzy Afro, and he wore eye makeup to put the hair bands of the '80s to shame. Add in a goofy swagger (maybe because of those white leather platform boots) and then you might be able to picture Zolotov.

He wasn't hateful; in fact, there were reports of how he had come into the world: parental neglect, forced to stay indoors, forbidden from making friends. His parents drilled him into practicing his instrument whenever he wasn't at school. Never did he receive praise for hard work or improving his skills.

As a teenager, he was able to stuff down his loneliness and shame, venturing out into the world of part-time work. After school, his side gig was giving saxophone lessons in the back of a guitar store. There were a lot of Greek families in his Queens, New York neighborhood, so he learned every Greek song he could find in the record stores and taught them to his students.

His sudden death—and likely murder—came as a shock to his swooning fans. He'd gained a new generation of devotees who loved his retro vibe and what they perceived as him sticking out his middle finger at the old-school musicians. The irony was that he had now become the musical establishment. No matter.

After turning their backs on the harsh non-melodic sounds of "free" jazz and looking for a return to sweetness and sentimentality, Zolotov's popularity went through the roof with the younger set. The hipsters took note and frizzed their own hair, donning suggestive T-shirts that proclaimed "Jerry Z, blow for me" with a full-body image of Zolotov pouring out sweat and laying out another one of his famous hyperextended notes.

Who was it, exactly, that decided they'd had too much of the glitz, the glamour, the fringes dripping with sequins, and that the Z man had to be taken out?

Becka's fascination with Russia started when she was nineteen.

At the time, she lived a mile further from Brighton Beach in a Brooklyn neighborhood called Flatlands. She used to play handball as a little kid; or rather, she *tried* to, since it was almost impossible to find a proper court. The adjoining neighborhoods by the ocean, Coney Island and Brighton and Manhattan Beaches, had courts, and they were all in use every weekend.

Handball was a big deal in the 1980s. Men, hordes of them, all shapes and ages and sizes, would wield callused hands and jump around the court, spitting curses and congratulations as the sweat shone off their buff bodies. Becka would ride her bike on the bumpy wooden boardwalk. Beyond a few slats that were a tripping hazard and replaced by lighter wood planks, she wondered if the boardwalk had ever been fully repaired. It was ancient, probably looking much the same as it did in the days of parasols and freak shows in the early 1900s.

As kids, Lizzy, Julie and Becka, three best friends, got together on Saturday mornings to ride their bikes and seek out a suitable wall to play handball on. They had pink spongy balls you could buy at any newsstand that weren't meant for the serious handball player. Eventually, they graduated to the hollow, more professional Spaldings (pronounced "Spaldeens" or else you were kicked out of the borough). Since these makeshift schoolyard courts were unevenly worn, the ball took unpredictable angles coming off the wall. But with the beach courts occupied from the crack of dawn, the schoolyards were the closest places they could find to play handball. There was one other location they could go to get the real experience, but it was a mile in the other direction. The campus at Brooklyn College, far removed from the sea air of Coney and Brighton, had installed smooth, new handball courts. The girls biked there when they felt like braving the heavily trafficked Ocean Avenue.

Perusing the boardwalk to watch a few games was a great way to occupy Becka's weekends, especially when her friends weren't available. The beachside courts thrummed with activity. She got to know the regulars by sight. Handball was an impressive cardio workout. The players were in glisteningly impressive shape, but of course, it wasn't an indicator of their overall health because they all smoked like chimneys.

Julie moved away and Lizzy went to a private college in Massachusetts. Becka stayed local and took the Nostrand Avenue bus to her Brooklyn College classes, but it was lonely without her friends. One particular Saturday morning in June, she found herself biking over to the courts to see if the handball scene was still the same as she remembered when she was a kid.

Her favorite court was the one at the boardwalk entrance on Ocean Parkway. She locked up her bike and started watching a game. It was packed. The guys were being extra rowdy to impress her. There was one guy in particular who was really acting up. He was

Russian and gorgeous. Becka's heart stopped the first time she saw him swing at a ball. He let out a string of foreign curse words when it went out of bounds and turned his head to spit off-court. That's when he caught a glimpse of Becka and smiled.

He told her his name was Pyotr Fisheleff. They started talking when he took breaks in between games, and she came to watch him every Saturday.

Pyotr was staying with his cousin Evgeny in Little Odessa and had learned English when he was a kid. He took a part-time job at the bagel and knish place right under the elevated train tracks on Coney Island Avenue. She only found that out because one powerfully hot Saturday morning, he had on a T-shirt that said "Best NY Bagels" in Hebrew lettering. When the sweat started to weigh down his shirt, he peeled it off and turned around to throw it aside. Becka's jaw dropped. She couldn't cover her mouth in time, and he saw her and winked. "You need bagels, yes?" he called over. He had eyes like black cherries. You couldn't see the difference between his pupils and his irises. "You come and see me. Here." And he held up the shirt and pointed to the logo. How could she not go there for her next sesame with scallion cream cheese?

They didn't really date; it was more like hanging out, taking strolls on the boardwalk and just getting to know each other. He said he had somebody back home and couldn't be her boyfriend, although it was clear he wanted to kiss her. Then she found out something amazing about him. He played the theremin.

Of course he would. Nobody even knew what that was. Becka only knew about the instrument because she was a music major at Brooklyn College. It was basically a radio transmitter that you "played" by intercepting the signal with your hands.

"How much longer do you have before you go back to St. Petersburg?" she asked him.

"Next Thursday."

Wow. That was a shock. Good thing she didn't start to have feelings for him.

"I didn't want to spoil our walk and talk about leaving," he said, not looking at her. "But if you're up to it, I'd like to play my theremin for you. Come up to my cousin's place?"

Evgeny lived above a restaurant in Little Odessa. It was a noisy neighborhood, and the apartment was narrow and dark. Pyotr slept on the couch. She saw all his belongings splayed out on a dresser in the hallway, including another bagel store T-shirt and two skinny cans of handballs, the real kind that hurt when you hit them. She couldn't pass up the chance to hear him play: to watch his hand delicately intercept the flow of air above the theremin to create music. And he didn't disappoint. He played a few classics like "Devil Moon" and "Tea for Two" and zoned in on every single note, even incorporating wavers and trills to give the songs more depth without overdoing it.

He was, in a word, a magician.

She slid her fingers over the base of the instrument. It was incredible to think you could produce these very eerie sounds with subtle hand movements while not touching anything. "Are you bringing it back home with you?" she asked.

"Yes. It comes completely apart. The antenna is the most delicate part, and I have foam packing to go around it."

Silently, she sighed. He saw her chest rise and fall. She wasn't fooling anybody. It had been almost two months and she was extremely attracted to him, but she knew this day was going to come. What was the point of getting involved?

"Will you be here to say goodbye? Evgeny's taking me to JFK on Thursday at six in the morning. I know it's a lot to ask...."

There was no question Becka would be there. Maybe she'd sneak in a kiss. She didn't really know what he meant by having somebody "back home." The way he looked at her, she wasn't too sure about it.

"I'll bring some bagels for a quick breakfast together," she promised. "You tell me what your favorite is, then I'll go back home and cry."

"I'll cry more."

Becka squeezed his hand. "See you then, Peter."

He perked up. Nobody called him that.

She gave him a broad smile, then turned to leave, blowing him a kiss.

When Becka got out to the street, she heard the window creak open above her.

"Becka!" he called down.

"What?"

"Toasted pumpernickel with a *leetle* butter."

Jeff Wright slammed both hands on the dining room table and stood abruptly. His eyes were slits and his face turned the color of a tomato. Becka expected to see steam coming from his ears. She had just delivered the news that he had received one too many calls from different women at work, and now she was done.

"You're leaving me, and you're—you're actually leaving the country? For *Russia*?"

Here comes the queen of dysregulated emotion, she thought. Why had it taken her so long to quit this relationship?

"One thing has nothing to do with the other, but yes." Becka got up and pointed her body to the door. There was no worry of his getting violent, but these tantrums often spilled over to his Cody, who'd be coming downstairs any minute now for his mom. Becka didn't want him to get yelled at just because Jeff was pissed at her. Poor kid. And she was starting to bond with him.

"My ex is on her way over," he said, as if this was an issue for Becka.

It wasn't; she and Suzanne were friends from grade school. Becka only started seeing Jeff a year after they got divorced, and only after she got Suzanne's blessings. But she'd laughed and told her, "Lots of luck!" and now Becka knew why.

"I have to get Cody ready and make sure his stuff is packed," he continued. "Your timing is impeccable."

Becka took her keys from her handbag.

"And what the hell are you going to Russia for, anyway? To get away from me?"

"I already told you, but of course, you don't listen. Because I've always wanted to go, and because my family is from there, and because of those bone records I told you about that, by the way, you think are so stupid, and for a million other reasons. It doesn't matter now, Jeff."

"But why are you breaking up with me?" He was truly perplexed.

"Why? The six months we've been going out, all those chicks from work always calling you, that's why. And you said you were 'so into' me? We're O-V-E-R."

The crunch of snow in Jeff's driveway told her that Suzanne's Prius was rolling in. Definitely time to leave.

Becka actually adored Suzanne (Jeff certainly didn't), but her arrival would put him more on edge. Becka had a new adventure awaiting her and was so, *so* ready to leave this chapter behind her.

"Hi, Becka!"

Suzanne was in the doorway, beautiful and beaming like always. Why Jeff left her, Becka could never understand, but she got the better end of the deal. Her freedom.

"Suzie!" she said, going in for a hug.

"What's up, gurrrrl?"

Cody came flying out of the house. The last thing Becka wanted at this point was somebody else's family dynamics. She had recently handled her own, and then her mom died.

"Listen, I'm going to Russia—" Becka began.

"What? When?"

Cody nearly knocked Suzanne over.

"I can't, gotta pack. Let me call you. Soon, I promise! Before I leave!"

She shot Jeff a mournful look and walked out forever.

Why did she want to travel to Russia? Just like her relationship with Jeff Wright, it was complicated.

The Motherland always called to her. She had an uncle who sent all the cousins and sons and daughters a skinny black loose-leaf book with their family history. The pictures were of Grandpapa (not Becka's; her father's) with his weary eyes and unkempt beard, a furred hat atop his head and heavy waistcoat pulling his thin frame down with the gravity of the past. The photos spoke to her through the ages. Her ancestors had come from Lvov, which at times was geographically part of Poland, or was it Ukraine? Then, of course, the bone records she'd learned about years before. That was another reason.

Becka wondered if the timing was right, though. A new president had just been voted in and a lot of questions were swirling about his relationship with the head of Russia. If she really wanted to go—and before things heated up too much and travel was restricted (or worse), before any time-honored ethnic pacts suddenly exploded—she needed to go now.

Of course, there was one more reason for her trip. She had found Pyotr Fisheleff online, her old boyfriend from the handball courts at Coney Island. They started talking again; nothing romantic, just friends reconnecting. It had been over twenty years. He wanted to see her and promised it would be a visit she'd never forget.

Becka got her first accordion back in seventh grade. They were so obscure that the best place, or maybe the only place, to get them in the '70s (unless you could afford a brand-new one) was from a pawn shop. But a 15-year-old girl couldn't go into pawn shops in New York City.

Lizzy was able to convince her stepdad, a sportswriter for the Daily News, to duck into a few pawn shops on the Lower East Side looking for an instrument for her best friend, Becka. "You'll have to take whatever he finds," Lizzy warned Becka. They thought it was hysterical that he would do this for her, carry around an accordion on the New York City subways, but it was really symbolic of his efforts to bond with his stepdaughter. She'd had a nasty time of it with her biological dad, who left in an alcoholic haze when she was very young.

It had taken a few months, but Becka came up with the cash through babysitting and running grocery errands for a few elderly residents in their apartment building.

One night, Lizzy knocked on Becka's door, and lo and behold, there was a beautiful, beat-up monster of an accordion that she could barely pick up. Becka's mother didn't know about any of this, and when she found out, she was very upset, mostly because she was out of the loop.

In elementary school orchestras in the 1970s, most people had never even heard an accordion on a record.

The only way would have been by picking through the albums at Tower Records or Colony Records or (slim chance) at your local record store. If you were really lucky, the store owner would play you a snippet on his clunky turntable behind the counter. But you'd have to pay for the album first.

She'd heard it growing up on the *Lawrence Welk Show*. Her mom had it on sometimes in the background while she was doing the dinner dishes.

What fascinated her about Lawrence Welk, besides his stiff way of speaking and his perpetual smile, was how he could play what was essentially a piano on its side and then, on top of that, create these flavorful chords from all the little buttons on it. And then, the cherry on the sundae: he could pull it apart and squeeze it together just right, imparting life into it and coaxing out music. Becka wanted one the very first time she saw it.

Becka held onto the accordion even after she outgrew it. It reminded her of being a kid and discovering music for the first time.

The kids at school made fun of her when she talked about watching *Lawrence Welk*. They said that anyone who played the accordion was a weirdo, which of course made her even more resolute. Now that she owned one, the next step was to ask her music teacher where to get cheap lessons.

The teacher arranged for Becka to take lessons with a local musician on Tuesdays after school for ten dollars an hour. By that time, she'd gotten a part-time job at a local hardware store and could afford it.

Her mother didn't hide her contempt and said she didn't know why Becka even wanted lessons. She'd never be able to make a living playing it, so why bother?

When Becka first mentioned her trip to Russia, Jeff literally laughed in her face. That was the icing on the breakup cake. On the ride home from his house that afternoon, as she cruised along on I-80 East, she got off an exit too soon.

Driving through Milford, with its beautiful lawns and stately homes, she saw sign after sign for yard sales. At a stop sign, she saw one that caught her eye. It read: "Everything Goes—Clothes, Furniture, and Music, Music, Music." *That's my kind of picking,* she thought. She found the house, parked at the back of a long line of cars and walked up the driveway.

People were pawing ferociously at the end tables and Queen Anne chairs. On the lawn stood several music stands, a table with a nice still-life assortment of old horns and saxes, a keyboard or two, and cartons of sheet music. As Becka got closer, she saw that one of the cartons had something with rows of buttons sticking up out of it. Shiny, pearly, sparkling in the sun. Could it be—?

It was a precious little Hohner Compadre concertina, a portable (if you were strong) accordion. If she could afford it, she decided she'd name this cutie Athena. The homeowner told her it was another two thousand wasted. Not the instrument (she reassured) but the lessons. And, she said, her son was nowhere closer to playing anything resembling music.

"What do you want for it?" Becka asked.

"You got cash?" the woman snapped back.

Oh Lord, please let me have enough money on me. Then she remembered cashing part of her overtime check a few days earlier.

"Two hundred twenty-five," Becka declared without flinching. It was going to be store-brand pasta again for weeks.

"It's yours."

Becka's face was hot and she couldn't look the seller in the eye. She could tell just by the iridescence on the buttons that this wasn't for some entry-level hobbyist. This was a two-thousand-dollar work of art.

Miraculously, it was the answer to Becka's prayers. She had asked Pyotr if he knew of any local musicians there to jam with. She was in luck; he had friends who played regularly. Her new compact concertina would be perfect to bring along.

When Becka got Athena home and gave her a more thorough check-up, she saw a few things that needed to be fixed before the trip, like replacing two of the internal reeds, unsticking a few buttons and getting a sturdy case for traveling. She still had about a month to do it and found somebody in New York City, which of course meant a day trip there and another full day to go pick it up, but there was no sense in offering to play with other *muzikanty* (musicians) and then having your instrument in less than tip-top shape.

Becka had some private lessons after school when she was younger, but when she declared her music major in college, she wanted to go deeper. One of the professors at the time, Al Florenci, gave lessons at a local music store. At her first lesson, he'd talked about his recent visit to Eastern Europe.

"Why there? Family?" she'd asked.

He paused his accordion mid-pump. They were working on the different modes, and Becka was having trouble memorizing them.

"No, I was tracking down some bone records," he said.

"Bone whats?"

"Bone records. Songs recorded onto X-ray films they used instead of vinyl. Well, originally, records were made out of shellac and other kinds of plastic. Anyway, the bone records were around when our records were banned in Russia. You never heard of them?"

"No. Sounds fascinating!"

He rested his instrument on a table. "So they couldn't listen to jazz there in the '20s all the way up to the '50s, and everything from the West became a big hot deal. They re-purposed old X-ray films, found a way to embed grooves for a stylus, and made bootleg records out of 'em. Go look 'em up, you'll see for yourself."

Becka never forgot that conversation. *Some day, I have to see one of these for myself.*

"Let's get back to the modes. We only have fifteen minutes left here and this old man is getting tired."

Now, years later, she was finally going to Mother Russia and could see one for herself, perhaps even buy one. The Cold War was long over, and there was no reason in the world that it should be difficult to find one and bring it home to cherish forever.

Becka obviously had a lot to learn.

As soon as Becka landed at Pulkovo International Airport in St. Petersburg, she realized how woefully unprepared she was for the cold. The mind-numbingly frigid air sucked the oxygen from her lungs and frosted her eyelashes. She felt like her eyelids would become fused together if she didn't cover her entire face with her scarf.

Finding her way outdoors to the taxi stand, she shuffled her way forward, eyes trained on the icy walkway. She expected to fall flat on her butt at any moment. Her leather messenger bag was strapped across her chest one way and the accordion case went the other way, marking her torso with a big canvas X. She pulled the suitcase behind her. Her gloves were set inside oversized floppy mittens, hampering her grip but keeping the cold away.

After threading his way through the line of cabs, he found her.

"Becka!" It was a beat-up old Dodge Aries K. Years since she'd seen one.

Their Facebook chats and Zoom calls were filled with cultural misunderstandings and lots of laughs. Over the better part of a year, she felt like they'd gotten to know one another pretty well. He seemed like a safe bet. Like he would look out for her.

If any of her friends had told her they were doing what she was doing right now, she'd have smacked them. Meeting some guy she hadn't seen since she was twenty and traveling to Russia to meet him sounded crazy even to her. What if he changed since their bagel days; what if he was a murderer or something?

Becka put her faith in the universe. Somehow she felt she could trust Pyotr. As her old Grandpa Morris would say, "Life without risk is like a dinner without paprika."

At the moment, she had no other choice. Pulkovo surrounded her and cars were about to run over the both of them. It was time to start her adventure.

Becka was grateful for the warm car that was waiting for her. Pyotr stepped out and ran over, almost knocking her down. After a few rounds of looking each other over and hugging, they rode back to her hotel an hour away.

"Aren't you going to come up to the room?" she asked coyly.

"No, not now. You go and freshen up. Take a nap if you need one, okay?"

What a relief.

"Meet me at the bar," he said to her, "when you're ready. No rush. I'll text you the address. It'll take you about thirty minutes to get there. Just let me know when you're leaving."

Once in the door, she was ecstatic to be able to take her own hot, soapy shower and a catnap. She needed it.

An hour later, the hotel helped her get a Yandex cab ride over to the bar. She found it packed with people spilling out into the night. The streets were lit like daytime, loud with laughter and yelling. Becka didn't understand anything they were saying, but it was definitely a party atmosphere.

She stepped inside the *Khoroshiy Vremena* ("Good Times") Bar, her nostrils assaulted by the oily smell of hops. It triggered something deep and sensual, a stark contrast to the bitter cold outside. She pushed her hood back. Her hair was a complete static show, but there was no time for preening.

"Here she is!" he said from a table in the back, waving her over. Though crowded and very noisy, his voice cut through easily.

She shuffled her boots on the soggy rug at the entrance and then moved slowly onto the laminate floor to avoid falling.

His smile could light the way for a harbor full of boats looking for their home. Becka was instantly attracted to him (again) but vowed to keep her feelings in check. She was trying to get a bone record and maybe visit the town where her great-grandfather had lived if there was time.

"Hello, Pyotr!" Before she could tug off her coat, he was standing behind her, guiding it off her shoulders. He smelled spicy, like bay rum. One of Becka's favorites. She was doomed.

"Oh my God, thank you. I was suffocating!" She huffed into the booth and scooted over to the wall. He had already gotten her a cup of hot chai. The foam on the top was a pattern of musical notes.

Clearly, this was part of his seduction plan.

"I went forward and got you the best chai you will ever taste." His eyes twinkled.

"And for that and many other things, I appreciate you." She twinkled back.

"Tell me more about why you want an X-ray record so badly. And let's talk about music! Where is your accordion?" He drew a flower on the table with the condensation from his drink (straight whiskey). The stem of the flower snaked over to her side of the table and ended in a heart.

Becka saw the writing on the wall. Or rather, the table. This was going to be one hell of a trip.

The conversation was flowing like honey. Unless Pyotr had been drinking since he left her at the hotel, he was only on his second beer, and it was apparently all the social lubrication he needed. They talked about the ridiculousness of social media and their favorite videos and reels, the ones that made them spit out their drinks.

"And then there's you guys!" she said, challenging him.

He looked at her with a question on his face. "What? The ones about life in Russia? Those *stoopid* memes?"

Becka puffed out her cheeks, buying a few seconds. "I just think they're hysterical."

"Yeah. Go make fun, my dear. And what if I laughed at you for the part of you that is Russian, hey? Your family tree and all that."

"You're not wrong. So what I chide you about, it's only with affection and bounces back to me."

He glugged another mouthful of beer and then reached for her hand. He flipped it over and, with his finger, made circles on her palm.

Becka blushed.

"So tell me, my accordion-playing American. Did you come from royalty? Because you sure look like a princess to me."

"I'm pretty sure that our ancestors were the village paupers, so no royalty here," she said. "But if they saw me today, they'd think I was rich. A billionaire." She looked at her palm. He had stopped making circles and cradled her hand.

"These hands."

She was exhausted but knew he was trying to start something.

"What about my hands?"

"Tell me how you learned to play jazz on that contraption, of all things!"

It was going to be a long night. They were only getting started. Chapter Two would undoubtedly happen back at the hotel.

Becka hoped he didn't have any early morning plans for them.

They were more than adequately hydrated and decided to head back to his apartment. As she found a place for her luggage and her concertina, she turned to ask him what side of the bed he preferred. She didn't get to ask.

"I have to go out soon. But only for an hour or two. When I get back, we will have the rest of the night together. If you want to stay here, which I hope you do. We'll get your stuff in the morning and you can cancel your hotel then."

She looked at him and weighed the prospect.

"Of course." It was the only thing to say under the circumstances. And she really wanted to. But where was he going out to, on a night like this, their first night together after the build-up of the past five months?

"Don't look at me like that, it's nothing!" He tried a smile. "I'll be back soon. I know you're tired. Start your sleeping without me and I'll slip back between the sheets in no time!"

This was a surprise. So was the question that came out of her mouth immediately after.

"So, where are you going?" It was hard to know what the boundaries were. He was really only her host for ten days, not her boyfriend. Not yet.

Pyotr licked the corner of his mouth. "I love it when you meddle."

"Got it. Sorry." *I guess.*

"No problem, my sweetheart. We eat, then I go."

Becka was craving carbs, lots of them, and the food Pyotr ordered in didn't disappoint. The blood-red beets seeped into the mashed turnips, making them pink. Thick chunks of boiled beef were almost too salty. The rye bread was some of the densest she'd ever seen and the taste was powerful and deep.

She watched him eat. Clearly, he enjoyed overindulging. Maybe he was thinking about other types of pleasure.

"I don't always eat this way or this much. But present company gives me an appetite to beat a band."

Becka smiled. "*The* band," she corrected him. It was adorable that he was trying on some Americanisms. This was why she agreed to try the beets. A cultural exchange.

"I tried beets once and gagged," she shared. 'But for you, I will give them another chance." She tucked a napkin under her collar.

Pyotr was just going to be a fling, apparently. Becka didn't think he had any grand expectations about her, either.

Becka would say yes to everything during this trip, and then, when she got back home, she'd find something special to send him for such a wonderful time.

Only now, she wondered where he was going that he couldn't tell her.

As promised, Pyotr was back in the apartment after an hour. He tried to come in quietly but Becka woke at the sound of the key in the door.

It was hard to fall back asleep now that she was in bed with a virtual stranger. She hoped this wasn't a mistake.

She flipped and flopped and kept rearranging her pillow.

"Why are you so jumpy?" he mumbled. "Aren't you tired?"

"Sorry, it's all so new to me. I'm excited, especially to finally meet you again after all these years."

"Mm, yes, that is pretty special." He lightly kissed her lips. "What is on your mind? What do you hope to accomplish here?"

She didn't know how to respond. She was expanding her horizons, experiencing another culture, and hopefully going to see a real bone record in the flesh, so to speak.

"Accomplish?"

Now they were both fully awake.

"Yes," he said. "You want that bone record, right? There's a joke in there somewhere, you know."

"I got that loud and clear, bud. But yeah, that was the motivation here. Oh, plus meeting you in person, of course."

"Anything else...?"

"Wait! Hear those sirens? Sounds just like home. In Brooklyn, we hear them all day, all night. Whining away."

"Your attention span is like the half-life of Moscovium," he said, a challenge in his tone.

"Ah. Element 115."

He sat back. "So you know about chemistry too. Brains *and* beauty!"

"Yes, well, my ex-boyfriend's son was—is?—a budding chemist. And he was always thrilled when a new element came on the scene. He called it something like 'the juice that powered the UFOs,' if you buy into that."

Pyotr smiled broadly. "I don't. But then again, I grew up in a culture of questionable news programs and misdirected truth. I discarded all of it. But let's get to that 'ex' situation, hmm?"

"What do you want to know? I was with somebody, we went out for around six months, and now he's toast."

He took a healthy gulp of rum from a paper cup on the nightstand. "Surely something happened in between?"

Becka matched him with a generous sip of a hearty Polish red that he had opened for the occasion. It was unexpectedly mellow.

"Yes, something did. It was a sprint, not a marathon. We didn't have the same interests, like his in other women. I mean, even from the get-go. He took calls from all these female co-workers who supposedly 'needed his help,' and he even cut short our dates to go be with them. I'm no fool. Not anymore." She raised her glass. "So, that's my tale. What about you?"

He took a slow, deep breath and let it out in a hiss.

"I was married," he said, reaching over to touch her hair. "She was the love of my life. I don't know if you believe in such things, but I make no apologies."

Becka nodded for him to continue.

"She fell ill after a lavish dinner at her boss's home that we attended. She got an infection in her kidney, went into sepsis, and.... Well."

"I'm so sorry. When did this happen?"

"Like two years ago. Life hasn't been the same. But on we go, right?" He took a long honk into a tissue and wiped his eyes.

She let it sit a bit. Her own woes didn't compare.

"Anyway, fun fact for you," he said, perking up. "Element 115? My uncle worked for the Joint Institute for Nuclear Research. He was on the team that discovered it. The Americans collaborated and they weren't keen on naming it after our capital, but we won. Small Soviet victory!" When he smiled, he had a dimple, but only on one side.

"That's a great conversation starter, isn't it?"

"And it's funny that you mention Moscovium."

"How so?" she asked.

It was very challenging being so close to him and curbing her growing desire. They hadn't really kissed yet. But Becka really wanted to hear more of that beautiful voice of his.

He continued with the history lesson. "It is my cousin's father-in-law who helped discover it with some other scientists in Dubna, which is about one and a half hours drive from Moscow. The thing about it is that it's a fleeting element. You only observe it by not observing it directly. Much like getting to know you."

He quickly scanned Becka's eyes and imperceptibly arched his perfect man-eyebrows at her. She knew this micro-expression to mean attraction. Her heart did a flop and she knew she was blushing. But they were both too tired to let the moment become more intimate. The time would come soon enough.

"There's something I want to show you." Pyotr went to another room and came back with a violin case. He beamed at her and unsnapped the case.

"I will tune it up. It will take a minute."

Becka held up her finger and scurried into the bathroom for a quick pee. When she came out, he was on the mattress, balanced on his knees, the bow cocked and ready to dig into the low G string. His elbow was pointing to the ceiling.

"Ready?"

He speared the bow into the strings and, one after the other, pulled forth a beautiful, aggressive chord. The notes hung in the air. He lingered on the highest string, then slid his way up to a high D, which he attacked and lent a very fast vibrato to.

He was obviously showing off. He grinned like a maniac and then started playing something familiar and incredibly fast.

"'Flight of the Bumblebee'?"

He nodded as he sawed away at the notes in a perfect frenzy.

"Do you know why I play this for you?" he asked, brow sweating and wrist flying with a death grip on the bow. "Can you guess?"

"I don't have the slightest idea."

"Bee, bumblebee, it's what means 'Deborah,' which was my mother's name."

"Oh. I see. Did she like this piece?"

He laughed, breaking the pace. "No, actually she hated it. Said it gave her a headache. But I play it now to honor her."

That was beautiful, Becka thought. Back in the US, a man would never say that for fear of being accused of having mommy issues. Pyotr didn't care how it sounded, and she found it sweet and endearing.

"Since we're getting to know each other, I want to tell you what happened to her."

Oh no, she thought.

He wiped his brow with a corner of the sheet and set down his instrument. Becka had never pictured a hot, naked fiddler before, and now she knew it would haunt her dreams forever.

His bunched-up smile with glossy eyes changed the mood. He was holding onto something very painful.

"It was bad enough that I saw my father beat up my mother when I was six...and then he left us. Thank God for that. However, when I was thirteen and had just learned the violin, this violin here, my mother was poisoned. My sister and I, we lost her and had to go live with her aunt in another city."

"Oh my God! Was it—did she go against the government or something?"

"Ha!" he shouted, making her jump. "No, nothing like that. You guys always think there is so much drama here in Russia and all these cover-ups. What about your own conspiracies?"

"You have a point. We have lots. Don't get me started."

He nodded. "Okay, then. She was poisoned by our neighbor, a very nice old lady who was clearly losing her, how you say, marbles. She thought my mother was having an affair with her husband and she brought over some soup."

"What!"

"You can probably find it online if you look. It was cabbage soup, and we were all going to have some, but my mother actually had about half a bowl of it before we got home from school. I came home to find her on the floor."

Becka couldn't imagine witnessing this at such a young age, coming home to find your mother on the floor, lifeless. It was heartbreaking.

"How did you know it was the soup?"

"Well, the other half of it was still on the kitchen table, so the police tested it. It was arsenic, which kills quickly and without a taste."

"I am so very sorry, Pyotr."

She didn't feel like making love anymore, but he had other ideas.

"Let me put away the fiddle. Did you like it, by the way?"

"I did. May your mother rest in peace."

"Now you do something for me."

"We getting back to cuddling?"

"Not yet. I want to hear something on your concertina, and I won't take no for an answer."

This was a new one. Playing concertina in the nude. The bellows could pinch something. So she put her underwear and tank top back on.

"Wait. A question." He looked serious.

"Okay...?"

"My mother. Do you think her last thought was how the soup tasted or that she was about to die?"

Becka let the instrument's straps slide down her arms and rested the concertina in her lap.

How can I answer this?

"No, I'm serious. Please." He gave a brief smile.

"I think she maybe loved the soup, and that was it."

"Let's hope so."

She started with the most obvious of song beginnings: the glissando that launched "Rhapsody in Blue." But she said she didn't do it justice and the poor Gershwin brothers must have been rolling around in their graves. Pyotr thought otherwise.

"Very nice!" he said, applauding.

"Musical interlude concluded," Becka declared, setting the instrument on a chair and mischievously pulling the tank top over her head.

What was most intriguing in their first deep kiss was how the sting of nicotine on the tongue could make her blood burn an amorous path through her veins; normally, it would have been something she recoiled from, but she couldn't get enough of the bitterness. She thirsted for it; she wanted to swallow everything about him, starting with his mouth. When the surprise of her ardor finally hit Pyotr, he took control of the situation. But Becka reversed it by asserting her wishes, which Pyotr was having none of. The constant shift in dynamics was apparently a heady aphrodisiac for them both.

Licks and moans and insistent rhythms finally resolved as the two of them lay drenched in sweat, equally tuckered out and in full enjoyment of the residual pulsations that began to subside. The difference between them in this post state was Becka did not smoke, and he lit another.

Pyotr shook out a Winston and offered her one.

"No thanks, never touch the stuff."

He regarded her skeptically. "Ah, but you always wondered how you would look with a cigarette drooping seductively from your lips. Tell me that isn't true."

Becka smiled. Maybe he knew her more than she realized.

The sun was straining in the crack between the heavy curtains. She got up to pull it aside. The rooftops here had a certain beauty, an architectural diversity that was lacking back home. For a split second, she envied his life, with all the visual treats dotting his skyline, the spires and terra cotta chimney stacks.

The silvery smoke from his Winston was slowly torturing her throat. Much as this classic display of masculinity was playing havoc with her hormones (he looked sexy smoking, which she hated to admit), she slid off the bed and stood by the window. “Do you mind if I open it just a bit?”

“Go right ahead. You’ll need to keep it open with a book.” He drew on his cigarette until it was done, not wasting a centimeter.

“So what shall we do today, my musical munchkin?”

She loved that this serious man could be silly, too. The guys she’d been with were perpetually overstressed and preoccupied with their imagined troubles in life. Jeff, for example. He was so spoiled. Try being six years old and seeing your father shot in a robbery. That’ll cure you of your pedestrian complaints.

“What about we take a stroll today and you show me your best parks? I need some fresh air.” She went over to the window and raised it above where the book was wedged. Breathing in the cold, dry air felt amazing.

“Okie dokie. And I’m sorry for polluting your space here. I always like one of these after sex.”

“Oh, is that how it is?”

“I don’t do this often, the sex, that is, so please don’t think less of me.”

"I don't know how that would be possible."

He burst out laughing. Another check in the plus column: humility. How hard was it going to be to leave him behind?

After a chilly walk through a neighborhood park and getting breakfast sandwiches (plus another scalding cup of chai) to bring back to his apartment, Pyotr had an idea.

"One of the last guys who was around when the bone records were made is still in St. Petersburg. We are kind of, uh, colleagues. Do you want to see if he's up for a visit?"

"You don't have to ask me twice. Absolutely!" Becka's eyes were shining.

He promised her that Leonid would be the definitive source.

"Can I take a photo of him and his collection?"

Pyotr lightly pinched her cheek like a grandpa. Everything he did was with affection. It was driving her crazy, in a good way.

"You'd have to ask him about taking photos. I don't see why not, but old paranoia dies hard."

Whatever Becka was able to find out about bone records was jotted down into a notebook. She added some questions just in case she would get to meet somebody like Leonid. And now it was happening.

The ride was nearly an hour, during which he revealed that he'd taken the whole week off to spend with her. When she first told him about her plans to visit, she hoped she wouldn't be completely on her own. But she also didn't know what "taking a week off" meant because she didn't know exactly what he did.

Becka could barely say "hello" and "thank you" in Russian. Now she had her very own tour guide.

Which came to a halt.

"He lives in that cottage over there." Pyotr gestured to a small, beaten-up structure across the street from some empty storefronts.

"Wait, what?" She held the notebook against her chest and felt a sheen of sweat coming over her face.

"He's a strange dude. It's better if you go alone. It'll be fine."

Maybe they should have planned on sightseeing instead.

"Should I even go? I mean, you're saying he's weird, so...."

"Ah. I kid. He's the one to talk to about these things, the last holdout. Trust me, he'll love you. Better get in there before he dies!"

"Very funny. He'll let me in? And you'll be where?"

"Right here. I'm sorry, but I won't be joining you. He's doing me a huge favor. We, uh, really don't get along."

Becka didn't move. She was trying to listen to her gut, which said to think this through.

"Okay, so I guess you want to know why." Pyotr stared out the window and thought about how drafty it was going to be waiting in the car.

"When my wife got sick, he told me to take her to a different doctor. I didn't listen, and when she died, he couldn't face me. So he's either mad at me for not listening to his advice or he's too upset about it to meet my eye."

"Oh God, I'm sorry to hear that. You want me to skip this, then?"

Becka said a quick prayer in her head, hoping he'd tell her no.

"Nonsense. Go knock his socks off. He's eccentric, but in a good way. You'll see. Take pictures if he says you can. Now go!"

The street was icy with puddles over them. Becka slowly shuffled her fake Uggs step by step. Her pink backpack was filled with all the essentials: pens, a camera with extra batteries, her notebook, and a copy of the definitive book on bone records, the one that cracked things wide open, which she hoped to get the old man to sign. He was one of five contributing authors, the only one in the group who was still alive.

A few things to remember about Leonid. She'd need to be quick with her questions, gracious for his time, and careful about going into sensitive territory like discussing the Cold War or current relations with the US, which weren't looking so healthy at the moment. This didn't mean she couldn't ask him anything controversial, but she'd have to keep an eye on his micro-expressions and back off the minute he turned stoic.

She reached the weathered door and knocked three times, each one louder than the next, as she gathered her courage. She turned around to look at Pyotr across the street. He nodded his approval.

The door inched open and an old man who looked like a once-handsome movie star (but with rotten teeth) greeted her effusively.

"You must be Becka!" His accent was as thick as sour cream. "Please come in!"

She saw him glance across at Pyotr's car and hike his hand slightly in acknowledgment.

The place smelled like pizza. This was a surprise.

He closed the door and placed his back against it, pushing until the latch engaged. "I like to cook every day. The stores, they give you crap!" His face lit up like a lantern.

Leonid was, to her surprise, very talkative. He was also a really good cook. The pizza had chunky mushrooms and fanned-out caramelized red onions. She would need mouthwash later.

"Tell me everything you want to know. I'll give you whatever I have. Oh, but not the records! Ha!"

"Yes, of course! By the way, thank you so much for having me come over. Pyotr said...."

"Ah, Pyotr! If he had only listened to me."

She looked down, waiting for him to continue and not knowing how to fill the space.

"And you are very welcome," he added. "The X-ray records, you know about them, da?"

"I do. And I'm supposedly buying one tomorrow if all goes well!"

Crap, I probably shouldn't have said that. But this wasn't 1952. It was okay to buy these things now, wasn't it?

"That is excellent news. I wonder what they have. If you get a chance to listen to any of them, I highly recommend it. There is a strange sound to them. I cannot describe it."

Leonid looked down and nodded like he was remembering something sad. “But now I would love to show you my collection.”

He jumped up with a grin and disappeared into another room. Becka stayed put and looked around. The room was filled with solid furniture covered in fabrics in huge geometrics, bold reds and golds, and one wall covered in frayed velvet wallpaper with fat royal blue stripes. Every window except the one with wallpaper was blanketed in black brocade curtains. The décor was designed for privacy and isolation. She felt for him.

He came back with a portfolio, which he set on the floor. He looked at her and smiled. “Wait! Do I have pizza in my teeth?”

What a strange question. He was delightful.

“None at all,” she said. “But speaking of food, do you mind if I go wash up? I don’t want to get sauce on your films.”

He pointed to the bathroom and she freshened up with soap that was heavy with lemongrass.

The low coffee table was covered in bone records when she got back. He had more of these than she knew existed. Names like Bing Crosby, Buddy Holly and Chubby Checker were written on labels that had lost their adhesiveness. One fell onto the rug.

“The Beatles? What is this one worth?”

“Why you think I have black curtains?”

Was that a joke?

“I kid you. Kind of. That’s over a million three, but it doesn’t matter, it’s not for sale. And fortunately for me, there is no paperwork on these ribs, so nobody knows I have them. And before you ask, I cannot play this or any of these for you, unfortunately."

Becka's heart sank. "Oh, okay. Can I ask why not?"

"My stylus is broken and this old man doesn't get out much anymore. If you don't use the right one, you can ruin the record forever."

"Understood. But maybe you can help answer some questions I have about these ribs, as you call them?"

"I'm waiting patiently, my dear. What a beauty, by the way. Pyotr struck it rich."

Becka laughed. "Well, he's kind of an old friend. We're having fun being together."

He smiled. "Of course. All natural. Your questions?"

Becka cracked open her notebook and started writing. She asked her top four questions; it wouldn't have been fair to make him answer too many. Why she hadn't thought of bringing a tape recorder, she had no idea, and her phone battery was almost gone. Between Leonid's slurry of anglicized Russian and his idioms and hand gestures, she had a hard time keeping up.

"What are you going to do with all these answers, tell me?"

"Maybe write an article somewhere. I write about diagnostic imaging for a few radiology journals. It keeps me in pizza."

"And your full-time job?"

She told him about her career and then about playing the accordion. He was very forlorn that she didn't bring Athena along.

"Pyotr could have brought his theremin and I could chime in with my fiddle," Leonid said. "I played under Pags' protégé, you know. What a maniac...."

"Paganini? Come on, you're old, but you're not that old!"

"Funny lady." He was flirting. "For his young student, silly. I played under Deyvid Popov in the Moscow State Symphony Orchestra. I was the first chair of the violins from 1962 to 1977."

Her jaw fell open.

"Don't fawn over me, please." He grinned. "I play—rather, played—decently, but he was insistent that I develop my own style. He said I was a '*zhopa*-kissing Paganini clown' and 'sickeningly derivative.' Ah, but that's a story for another day."

Becka could have stayed for hours or even days. For every question, he had three great stories. But the sun was starting to cast long lines across the road outside. There was no exhaust coming from Pyotr's car, which meant he was conserving gas and getting cold.

The visit had all the makings of a great article. Maybe she could pitch the story to one of the tech journals or a music publication. She'd have to look into it when she got back home.

As she stepped out into the frigid air, Leonid rubbed her shoulders and said goodbye. She turned and hugged him. "If I get something published, I'll send it to you."

"Yes, wonderful. And good luck with your future purchase. Bone records have a way of changing one's life."

The next day, Pyotr had more good news for Becka about bone records.

"Ready to buy your own?"

They were lying in bed, flanks touching. He started kissing her shoulder with loud smacks.

"I am, but not if you keep this up," Becka said.

"Okay, I'll stop, but just for now."

"Am I on my own again, like with Leonid?" She got out of bed and stepped into his tiny shower. He followed.

"You are on your very own, but I'll be nearby. Not as near as I am now, though."

Pyotr dropped her off by a series of buildings with soaring spires and jewel-toned tiles. But she didn't see any record shops around. She turned to ask him where to go and saw him reach over to roll down his window. "Keep walking," he advised. "In two blocks—don't worry, they're short—you will see a school with beautiful black iron fencing. Here you will be."

"I'll be where?" she asked.

"You'll be right where you need to."

"But how will I know where the store is?"

Pyotr shook his head and laughed, then dramatically blew her a kiss. "I will pick you up right here in two hours. No matter what, don't be late."

With the blast of his unmufflered car, he was gone.

The chill sliced through her scarf. Lizzy had knitted it for her; it was her maiden voyage into a new hobby. It was lumpy and let the cold in. Becka wrapped it around her neck a few times and kept her chin down to handle the cold.

Becka wanted to take pictures of the beautiful buildings she passed, but Pyotr had warned her of all the security cameras. ("What makes you think it's any different in the US?" she'd asked him.) She'd have to commit the architecture to memory.

Two blocks felt like ten. She leaned into the wind and peered up occasionally to scout for the store Pyotr described. She'd have to walk back this way in two hours when it might be even colder, but at least the wind should be at her back.

Several yards away, Becka saw a slight clearing between buildings with a short, squat building and an iron fence. The building was set up like a storefront with a mass of potted plants and garden flags in front. What lush greenery could possibly exist in this frigid country, she wondered.

Becka stepped up to the door and gave a small, quiet knock.

Nothing.

She looked at her phone and considered calling Pyotr. Then she knocked again.

This time, the door swung open. A woman with long blue hair and a cigarette dangling from her lips gestured to Becka with long, slender fingers. "Come!" she said through her teeth, biting down to keep her cigarette in place.

"Hi, um, Pyotr Fish—"

"Yes, yes!" she said between puffs. "Fisheleff. Becka, yes? Come in."

Happy to get out of the cold, Becka stepped inside and unwound her scarf. The smoker flung the door closed behind her, then set her cigarette into an ashtray. The table had bags of soil, piles of colored gravel and half-wrapped bouquets of flowers. Baby's breath and green Styrofoam were everywhere. The place would have smelled great except for the cigarette smoke. Becka didn't care, she was warm.

She stuck her hand out. "Thank you. I'm Becka, and you are?"

"It's not important."

Oh, it's like that. She stiffened up. Was she in danger?

"Ha! That look in your eyes! I'm just kidding! You can call me Sofia."

Becka doubted it was her real name, but no matter.

"Sofia, your gardening shop is beautiful! But where—"

Sofia removed the filterless cigarette from her dry lips and waved her hand. "Come with me. The back room has all the best plants."

Becka was nearly in love with Pyotr. At the very least, they were good friends. But could she trust him about this woman? What if Becka were to quietly disappear among the spruce cuttings?

"I read your mind, Miss. You are totally one-hundred percents safe with me. I have the only certified nursery in the city, and I wouldn't risk your time, much less my time, on something I could not produce for my customer. Come."

They went down a staircase and entered a room that felt soundproof. The walls were institutional gray and a few dying plants hung haphazardly from wall brackets. This was not a place where green things grew.

"I know what you came for. So let me tell you a little story."

Becka was getting more nervous as the seconds clicked by. Then Sofia took her hand and looked deeply into her eyes. The same look Pyotr had graced her with. Either she was about to tell Becka a state secret or the seduction timeline was even shorter in Russia. She opted for the second possibility because the first was too terrifying.

"Let's proceed to the inner room. The best leaves are here!" Without missing a beat, Sofia turned and slipped into an interior room. Becka thought they were in the inside room, but apparently not. It was like the nesting dolls...one inside the next inside the next.

"Ahh." Sofia's chest deflated and she looked more relaxed. "We can talk here."

She gently slid open the topmost drawer of an impossibly long cabinet. Each drawer had a delicate metal label; the top drawer said *A-Б* in faint lettering, but most of the other labels were missing. People used to keep large-format film in cabinets like these, but no more. Everything was digital now, except in this strange, specialized world of clandestine X-ray records.

"Here are the films you have traveled so far to see. I hope it makes your trip worthwhile." She looked at Becka, her eyes dewy. There was definitely a vibe, and for a moment, Becka felt sad for her that the attraction was not mutual. She seemed like a person well-accustomed to a life without love.

Sofia scanned the contents of the top drawer. Then she pulled out the next drawer down, then the next, and finally the one at the bottom of the cabinet. "Here."

Becka knew quite a bit about medical imaging but had never seen films with tiny concentric grooves worn in them. Images of femurs and ribs and fingers filled her view.

Sofia felt her way to the last one and picked out the one at the bottom of the pile. It was encased in a yellowed archival envelope. Not a very scientific method of protecting something so rare, Becka thought.

"What's this?" Becka asked.

Sofia found a stool and rolled herself over. "Sit and be comfortable. You are going to be quite surprised by this story. Perhaps shocked."

She lit another cigarette. There was no air circulation, and the films definitely shouldn't be exposed to smoke. Becka wouldn't dare bring this up to Sofia, though, whose compact, muscular frame could probably rip Becka's head from her neck and then stuff her inside one of the walls if her favor turned to rage. Best to keep quiet.

"This particular film—"

Sofia placed the lit cigarette on a platter behind her and donned thick rubber gloves. Then she removed the film that was inside the yellow envelope marked *Polka Dots + Moonbeams.*

"Oh my God, is this with Jimmy Heusen? It's one of my favorites!"

"Yes. This is the only one that is left. There were three, but one was destroyed when Stalin's castle was burned and one was bought."

"Oh?"

"By an American. Like you."

Becka still didn't catch the significance of this particular X-ray. She squinted and then cocked her head.

Sofia blew out a cloud of smoke with a laugh. "Hold on, let me say what it is, and then you will know why I made sure you are seated."

She flashed her eyes at Becka, who instinctively clasped at her V-neck. Was her cleavage showing, she wondered?

"This is the X-ray of Stalin's little girl."

"Oh, I think I've heard of her," Becka replied. "Pretty fascinating that you have this."

"No, not the daughter you've read about. A child. A baby. She died before she reached the age of two. Her name was Uliana."

Becka stared blankly as Sofia pulled the film from its casing.

"She was killed. Poor thing. Nobody should go through what she did."

Becka wasn't piecing this together yet. Sofia took a draw of nicotine and went on.

"See these broken bones? Abused. A child, a baby. It is tragic. Nobody was supposed to know. The hospital workers and the nurses and even the doctor—

many of them disappeared 'mysteriously.' The authorities have no idea who did it. There were too many officers and soldiers constantly in and out of there. Probably hundreds of people had access to the wing that the little girl slept in."

Becka's eyes watered.

"They told the press that the child slipped away from a terrible disease. But little Uliana was as healthy as a pony."

Both women fell silent, sharing a moment of reflection.

"So you said aside from the one that was destroyed in the castle and this one here, somebody in the US actually owns the last Uliana X-ray record?"

"Well, yes. It was purchased by an American musician."

Becka could only imagine the kind of deep pockets a person would need to have to be able to afford such a controversial—maybe even dangerous—piece of history.

"So, what instrument does this musician play?"

"Did. What *did* he play."

"Oh, okay. I wonder if I know of him."

"Probably, my dear. In fact, he was in the news last week. Supposedly a suicide—he 'fell off a bridge'—but we all know it was murder. You might have heard of him. Jerry Zolotov."

Becka didn't expect this revelation and her brain circuitry hunted in vain for a response.

"Either another bone record collector wanted it or it's the government," she told Becka. "It's not because of this Cold War business, but because there is still national shame over Stalin and the truth about this child's death that somebody needs to stay hidden."

Three long *BLAAT*s sounded right outside the door. It had been more than two hours since Pyotr dropped Becka off. He wasn't even supposed to come up to the store, or at least, that's what he'd told her.

"I have to get going, Sofia, but thank you for showing this to me."

"Wait. I can sell you a different bone record if you want one. This one, of course, is not for sale." Sofia returned the baby bone record to its envelope and then to its reinforced steel drawer.

Becka could sense Pyotr's growing impatience. She'd not seen him upset yet, but she had the feeling she was about to.

Still, it was the chance of a lifetime, if she could even afford this record.

"What's the song on this other film?" Becka asked, pointing to another envelope.

"This little one? Ah, this one I can sell." She pulled it out to show Becka. "It's 'I've Got You Under My Skin' by Dinah Shore. It's a bit tinny, but it swings."

Spoken like a true jazz lover. Becka took a very deep breath and expelled it loudly. Dinah Shore? It wasn't going to be cheap. But she had to know.

"How much?"

"Seven hundred fifty, US."

Becka pulled back. "Whoa!"

"You can pay it off when you get back home. I think Pyotr told you about me, yes? So you already know I only work with authentic artifacts. There is a way to do it that protects me. I would ask you to take that route."

Sofia explained that she sold expensive "out of print" books on different topics that her clients bought online. They were actually phantom books with very little text. The royalties would be paid to Sofia in a purchase that looked legit. A physical book would be sent to Becka to complete the sale, but it would only be fit to keep a campfire going.

"I have some books on gardening, one on parenting and one about animals."

Becka had to seal the deal and bolt. "How about animals?"

She handed Becka a pre-printed card with the title of the book: *A Biologic Presentation of the Fauna of the Continent of South America* ("hand-signed by Charles Darwin" to justify the price). Sounded like a bunch of baloney, which it was.

"I am letting you walk out of here without paying me, with the promise that you will do so through your book purchase. So we have to kind of trust each other, yes?"

Becka was a natural-born cynic, but for some reason, she trusted this woman.

"You got it." Becka was helping launder money and probably breaking a few US and international laws, but she was buying a book that she would actually receive and be able to hold in her hot little hands. It would be a standard, normal-looking transaction and she felt she could take her chances. It would make her one of the rare jazz lovers who owned an honest-to-goodness bone record, a thought that made her almost salivate.

Congrats, Becka, you have now committed a crime while visiting Russia. I hope you like it in the Gulag.

Instinct took over and she kissed Sofia on both cheeks. "I really have to get going. Thank you."

Sofia looked into her eyes once more, this time smiling. "Yes. Sure. Let me show you how to get back out of here."

Becka scrambled out the door with her very own reinforced manila envelope. Pyotr leaned over from the driver's seat and held her door open like a getaway car.

"My dear...."

"I know, I went over the two hours. Sorry, sorry!"

He shook his head and smiled. "You'll have my kisses later. Let's get out of here."

Pyotr fussed with a lock of Becka's hair. "Are you ready to play?" he asked.

She knew this question wasn't meant coyly. It was the day Athena got to see Mother Russia.

Pyotr had arranged for Becka to sit in with a bunch of his friends who were klezmer players. She'd brought her instrument just for this occasion, but that didn't mean she wasn't nervous about it. She was not a pro and didn't have much experience playing that traditional Jewish music from Eastern Europe.

"*Raz Dva Tri Kachat.*"

She waved away a cloud of his smoke. "I'm supposed to know what that is?"

"It's their name, One Two Three Swing. They're a lot of fun. And don't worry, because your little squeezebox," he said, pinching her arm, "will do just fine. They're all very friendly. They won't bite like I will." He wriggled his eyebrows.

"Okay, but nothing crazy. Remember I told you that I played in a small community band? We did some retirement homes and synagogues and I played maybe a handful of klezmer songs, but I'm not really good. You heard me play. I mean, this isn't false modesty."

Becka envisioned making a fool of herself. She had no business calling herself a musician! Pyotr's friends would laugh hysterically and surely her ancestors roll over in their graves.

"Stop it! You are better than you say." Pyotr kissed her hand and held it to his cheek. "It's for fun, and you'll have a great story to tell when you get back home."

There was no way out of this without making Pyotr look bad. Maybe it would be fun and she was worrying over nothing.

"Okay. When in St. Petersburg."

"Ah! There's my sweet little honey-waffle."

"Do we know what they're going to play? Do they usually do the same songs?"

Pyotr laughed. "Are you a musician or an accountant, Becka? They're going to play whatever they play. Stop being so nervous. Now go pack up Athena and let's go to dinner. We'll head out straight from there."

It was eight-thirty. A bout of nerves hit Becka between the eyes and she felt a headache coming on.

She figured they'd be going into someone's grimy basement in an isolated corner of town. Instead, they walked into a dry cleaners. She tilted her head and asked Pyotr, "So, you need some pants pressed?"

"In the back. The best jazz is always in the back of stores."

She followed him through the dry cleaning establishment, coughing as the chemicals caught in her throat. "They keep this place open after hours?"

Pyotr grabbed her hand without looking back, leading her forward through the forest of hanging plastic bags weighted with pants and suits. "Yes, they trust that jazz musicians aren't going to steal somebody's, how you say, *skanky* polyester suit." He gave her hand an affectionate squeeze.

Becka was about to participate in her first Russian jam session. Would she hold up with the more seasoned players?

As they got through the whooshing plastic bags, Becka heard the crash of a symbol, then laughter.

They made their way out of the shop (the chemical smell was mostly gone, but only because a small window had been propped open with a splintered four-by-four) and into a large room with flickering fluorescent lights. *That'll be distracting.* Then she started worrying about everything all over again. Pyotr squeezed her hand tighter, as if he was reading her mind.

They walked into a group of people pushing each other around, screaming with laughter.

"Guys and womens!" Pyotr suddenly proclaimed. "This is Becka, who I told you about. Preeminent jazz concertinist all the way from Brighton Beach, Brooklyn!"

Becka pushed past her social phobia and pretended to remove her hat while going into a deep bow. They clapped. *This is not so bad. I can do this.*

"Welcome, Miss Becka!" A skinny blond man with an uneven black beard gave her a toothy smile.

"Thanks to the gods, we have our melody line!" a woman setting up drums shouted.

Pyotr found a chair along the back wall. Becka couldn't imagine why the proprietor didn't use the extra space to expand his business. "Just pretend I'm not here!" Pyotr told them. "I will watch and listen very carefully, especially that cute girl on the concertina." He shot Becka a meaningful look and pursed his lips.

"Are we playing to a real audience or just for kicks?" she asked the drummer.

"Well, both," the drummer responded. "Besides you, we invited our usual gang of friends who come to all our performances."

Becka nodded. "Well, I'll do my best not to let you down."

"Ah, nonsense. I'm sure you play like a beast. And by the way, I'm Minda," the drummer said, extending her hand.

They were a lively bunch, but at least she knew she was among friends. She threw her fate to the winds and slipped her hands into Athena's straps.

It wasn't a quiet instrument and there was no use trying to play timidly. To loosen up, Becka jumped into a quick Yiddish tune, pulling Athena like taffy. *Ah, there's my center*, she thought. All good.

Nobody looked up or commented on her playing. Instead, they fell in step with Becka's song. Avi, the clarinetist, harmonized with her notes, filling in the open spots. The keyboardist (Becka couldn't fathom how they'd shoved a piano in there) launched into a few soft arpeggios followed by a series of jaunty chords. He was the oldest of the group, probably pushing sixty. As he looked at Becka, still playing, a huge smile cracked his face. He tipped his head toward Pyotr and nodded in approval.

"Okay, everybody!" Minda silenced her cymbal. "The crowd should be starting to *treekle* in very shortly. Here we go!"

Oh crap, Becka thought. *It's now or never*. Seeing no sheet music around, she realized she'd just have to wing it. It wasn't like there were going to be any talent scouts around, and the audience would eventually be properly socially lubricated.

The "gang" Minda had referred to started piling in. As they shuffled into noisy metal chairs, the musicians ran through fragments of some Great American

Songbook tunes. Avi gave Becka another nod, appreciating that she could hold her own. They probably shared some lineage between them anyway, so Gershwin was as much in her blood as his.

Becka didn't know why Pyotr thought it would be an all-klezmer set, but he was wrong. Thank God for the songs she could play in her sleep, like "Tea for Two" and "Someone to Watch Over Me," which sounded weird on a concertina, but at least they were familiar tunes.

If there were any fire department occupancy maximums in the room, they were now surely surpassed. The heat in the room was almost unbearable, and Becka was pouring with sweat. Luckily, she'd worn several layers and could peel down to her tank top, which, when that eventuality came, solicited a bug-eyed stare from both Pyotr and Avi.

She smiled and closed her eyes, pumping Athena into an assertive melody and bopping her head. They were in the middle of "Do It Again." Each time the words "no, no, no, no, NO...do it again!" came around, all the men in the room screamed out the lyrics. Everybody was doubled over in hysterics. Athena was getting in some great little riffs, many of them out of tune, but nobody cared.

Pyotr had cleared a few chairs and stood on one as some other guy handed him a stick. (It looked like a billy club, but Becka couldn't be sure.) A skylight she hadn't noticed was being pried open. With the stick in place, it let in a blast of chilled air as the steam in the room was sucked out.

Becka grabbed her bottled water and drained it. Pyotr smiled at her and put a finger to his lips, then slipped out into the dry cleaners. He took a cold can of Diet Coke from the refrigerator in the main office and came back into the room, but as he did, the guy who'd handed him the stick came around in front of him. The musicians had migrated to the bebop end of things and were now swirling into one of Becka's favorites, Coltrane's take on "My Favorite Things." This was the most fun she'd had since the time she cut junior high to see "Singing in the Rain" on the big screen at Radio City Music Hall. Maybe even more fun.

She wasn't paying much attention to Pyotr, but out of the corner of her eye, she noticed this guy, who had a nasty red beard and was very tall, cornering Pyotr. The goon then tossed a chair out of his way and stormed back into the dry cleaners. Whatever was going on didn't look kosher.

She looked around at her new friends. Nobody seemed particularly bothered, so she kept playing. Then they heard, "Hey, *mudak*! Watch where you're going!" The musicians picked up the pace with "April in Paris" but turned their attention to the back of the room where the scuffle was.

As Pyotr and Red Beard slipped back into the store, in came a new musician, late to the party but welcomed with cheers. She rolled a table into the room with some sort of contraption on it. People stood on chairs to watch her. Somebody yelled, "Thank God you're here!" It looked like an old radio with two horizontal rods coming out of the top of it. Now Becka remembered. She'd seen a theremin years ago when she first met Pyotr, and he played it for her at his cousin's apartment. Today she would get to jam with a theremin, which, for most musicians, was unheard of.

As the theremin player bowed and gave a few quick hugs around the room, Pyotr came back in, this time without his "companion." He shot her a look and gave a thumbs-up. Becka nodded and took the solo that Avi, dripping in sweat, handed over to her. The band was generous that way, spreading solos around for every song.

The audience's joy fed into the overall vibe of the moment. When the theremin was set up, the player, a beautiful woman of about seventy with glossy platinum hair, took her solo right smack in the middle of a song. This obviously wasn't the first time the other players yielded to a theremin, but for Becka, it was an astounding thing to watch. Emotion overtook her, and a few tears tumbled down her cheeks.

When the theremin was done, chairs were cleared on the right side of the room for a makeshift dance floor, where the audience members jumped around, spilling liquor on each other. The floor was getting sticky. It was going to be treacherous to navigate their way out of there later, and the place would need to be cleaned up. It was one thing to raid the owner's fridge (Becka would leave money for the Diet Coke), but another thing to trash his back room.

Avi turned his sax upside down and shook the saliva from the bell, then called out, "Last song!" and led the way into the schmaltzy classic, "Europa." What place a concertina had in this song, Becka couldn't fathom, but by this point, she knew she could fake her way through anything. Nobody had kicked her out and chords were chords. Little Athena had held her own.

Four long songs later (Avi lied), they were winding up the last chorus, at least she hoped, of "The Girl from Ipanema." The guys in the audience formed a chorus line and were making up their own lyrics like "short and fat and bald and stupid, the guy from Ipanema comes waddling..." and it was hard to keep from collapsing because everybody was laughing so hard. She desperately hoped someone was recording this on their phone.

It turned out that they'd raised quite a bit of money for the evening. She didn't fully understand their monetary system, but it looked like a few wads of paper notes and lots of jangling coins had filled up a cigar box that a skinny young woman at the back of the room had collected. Becka didn't notice her before, which reminded her of the bearded wonder who was up in Pyotr's face earlier and left. He certainly wasn't there for the music, but he was very upset about something.

♪

As the audience members started to leave in a mishmash of chairs, Avi found his way to their newest musician.

"Miss Becka?"

"Yes?"

"How to say. Pyotr is lucky people. And you play good." A slight blush followed his words.

"You do, too," she said, smiling. "Thank you for inviting me to play." Then she gave him a hug.

"If you are ever here in your future...." he began.

"I will look for the handsome saxophone player who killed it on 'Europa.'"

Another blush.

She said her goodbyes to the rest of the band. She was going to miss them. The bonding that happens when people make music together, even when they don't speak the same language, was plain and simple magic.

Athena had rocked out like a pro. The little squeezebox was more versatile than Becka gave her credit for. Klezmer and Gershwin? What a trouper.

She gave a quick wipe to take the sweat and essence of vodka off Athena. A better cleaning would be needed. She zipped up the case and crossed her body with the shoulder strap.

"Ready?" Pyotr asked.

"Don't we stay to help clean up?"

"You get a pass. They were mesmerized."

"Thanks, but it's only right. We really should."

"No," he said. "They told me to take you back to the hotel, possibly with some *pelmeni* for our last night together."

"Some what?"

"Meat dumplings."

Just then, he pulled her in for a hot kiss. Becka was going to miss a lot about Russia.

They got to the hotel and she really needed a shower. Not a sexy one, just a good old-fashioned sudsing.

"I'm coming in, okee?" he asked playfully.

How can I say no?

A half-hour later, they were cooling off under the sheets. Pyotr stubbed out a Winston.

"You should really quit, you know," Becka mentioned.

"Mmm hmm. Don't worry about me."

"But I do," she said, pouting.

"Well, I hope I don't have to go out again tonight," he said, changing the subject.

Becka sat up. "Why would you?"

"Long story, no need to tell it."

That was a bit of a surprise, his tone and what he said. Not cool. Was that who he was? A guy who shared things with his lovers on a need-to-know basis? Couldn't they at least have a nice sultry wind-down before he had to get back in the swing of whatever illicit things he was probably doing?

"That came out wrong," he insisted.

"So then tell me what you meant."

"Just that, well, there are details that don't impact us."

Here I go, she thought. "If you're going to leave my side for one second tonight, it does impact us. Pyotr. I want you all to myself."

"You're right," he said, nuzzling her shoulder.

"But I need to ask you something else."

Now he sat up. This night wasn't going to turn out the way she'd fantasized.

"Yes, my waffle. Tell me. Ask me."

She inhaled slowly, letting her chest rise. He put her finger in his mouth and bit gently to lighten the mood. She ruffled his hair. He smelled like raisins. Deep, dark, delicious. But ask, she must.

"Is this about that guy who came into the club tonight?"

"I'm afraid it is."

"Who is he?" she asked.

Pyotr reached over to his pack of cigarettes and shook out a new one.

"His name is Silvan Sloane. He is a broker. And I am in the market for the things he brokers."

What was she, in the middle of a Jim Schetz thriller or something?

And heeere we go. "For what *things*?"

A puff of smoke drifted toward the ceiling. "I buy black market items like computers. I scrub them clean and sell them back to schools. To help the kids."

She wondered if there was a sign around her neck that said "lie to me."

"And why was he mad at you?"

"I promised him I'd pay for an upcoming order. His prices are very high. I don't have enough float."

This was going to have to do. She was sorry she asked and just wanted to get back to wherever they were right before they started talking about this Silvan Sloane person.

Becka stretched out her arm and pulled him closer. "Doing it 'for the kids' sounds good enough to me," she fibbed. "But I'm just...so cold. You wouldn't let your girlfriend freeze to death in a country she didn't even live in, would you?"

“What shall we do today? It’s your last full day in the Motherland. I want it to be special.”

Pyotr reached over to the nightstand and stubbed out his cigarette. He leaned over Becka, his hair getting in their eyes. The kiss that followed was long and sensual. Maybe they didn’t have to get out of bed today.

Then she remembered he had mentioned leaving to go somewhere else.

“Did you end up going out during the night? I must have been asleep if you did.”

He pulled away and sat up. He was naked and, at the moment, very impressive.

“Ah, yes. I did. But do you trust me?”

She hated being asked that. It usually meant a lie was coming.

“Okay....”

“I see you’re not convinced. However, it is best that I don’t tell you. But I swear on my mother’s eyes and my father’s name, that pig, it was not another woman.”

It would be very American of her to frown, pull the sheets up around her and ask what the other woman’s name was. On the other hand, she didn’t know why, but she believed him.

She looked away from his beautiful body (although it was difficult) and groaned. “Why even tell me this? Why can’t you be like other guys and just make something up?”

"It's just my work. I'm not being unkind, but the less you know, the better—that kind of thing."

"Are you in trouble? Is anyone going to be following us?"

"I don't think so."

Her heart protested in a hard thump. "Pyotr! You don't *think* so? What if they are? I gotta change my flight and get out of here."

He reached out for her leg and caressed her calf. Then he took her foot and masterfully stroked it, applying increased pressure on the soles and the ball of the foot. It felt good. She snatched it back.

"Tell me all of it, or I'm leaving."

"Before or after we make love again?"

She grabbed a pillow and smacked him.

"Okay. There are people..." he began.

Oh shit.

"People who want one of the Stalin records," he continued. "Sofia told you, yes?"

Becka nodded.

"Stop worrying. We both know you don't have it, and you couldn't afford it even if I gave you all my money. We're talking more than the two-plus mill Jerry Zolotov paid for his."

"Oh great," Becka said. "Tell me that my record caught somebody's attention and I'm just going to quietly kill myself here in your bed."

"No, don't do that! It's nothing like that." He went for a cigarette, then changed his mind. "Now that Zolotov is dead, the price has gone through the roof. These people, my, uh, colleagues, know the other ones

Sofia has are worth almost nothing. Dinah Shore? Come on. Nobody gives the crap."

Praise the Lord. Her head dropped and she let out a huff. Then she realized something else.

"Hold on. Somebody already knows I bought that one?"

"Yes, but not because they were following you. They weren't. Sofia's transactions are recorded on a restricted database. They are not the bad guys, though. These are friends of mine. They're collectors too. They're watching to see who comes out of the woodwork looking for Zolotov's bone record. Whoever it is will be sniffing around for it pretty soon if not already doing so."

"Is Sofia in danger?"

"See, I told you too much. I doubt she is, unless these thugs can't get their hands on Zolotov's record in the States."

He stroked her arm and tugged at the sheet that covered up her front. "Sofia knows the risks she's taking by selling the records. Even letting you meet with her was something she had to weigh. But once I told her about you, she was fine."

"But these aren't illegal now. Why all the intrigue?"

"I'm not going to tell you how Sofia came in possession of them...."

"Oh, I see." She didn't.

"Don't worry, she didn't steal them. The people who owned them before, well, now it seems they want them back. A few of the bones have become extremely valuable."

"Then what did you say about me to make her trust me?"

"That you were—are—beautiful and innocent."

A ring of warmth traveled down Becka's body. She looked over at him, all stretched out next to her and so very naked.

She wanted to ask *so that took you all night?* but refrained.

"Sofia and I and a few of our mutual friends talked about what we could expect to happen...mostly about how she could keep her store safe from 'curious' people."

"That sounds like a scary discussion. And you still didn't say when you got back in."

"Ha! You know how it is when Russian men get together to talk. What should take ten minutes takes two hours. I'm so sorry I left you alone."

Becka was confused, as was probably his intention. Still, she was going to be gone in less than twenty-four hours, and with Miss Dinah valued at practically nothing (though why she was asked to pay $750 was beyond her), she supposedly had nothing to worry about.

"Sofia said I could get a cardboard tube at the postal service to protect my record. Now that I know it's worth bupkis, I kind of feel I got fleeced."

"Well...a promise is a promise, right? I found you a person who sells them and you got what you came here for."

"True. And the record is worth something in terms of the jazz world. As long as it's authentic."

Pyotr nodded. "Yes, cross my heart, it is."

She would have to write a few articles and work overtime at the hospital to pay herself back for it.

"Okay, so let's do this. A quick shower"—his eyebrows shot up devilishly—"and a jaunt in my jalopy out to the PO to get your packing tube, then my choice of where to visit for your last day. The St. Catherine Palace Gardens. You will find it spectacular."

"Throw in lunch somewhere that doesn't serve borscht and you've got yourself a deal."

Pyotr was right; the gardens were spectacular, with baths, caves and the beautifully ornate architecture of St. Catherine's Palace. They crammed a lot into their morning.

Becka didn't have much to pack. Athena would be hand-carried onto the plane just like before. The cardboard tube containing the bone record slid easily into her knapsack. Her suitcase would be checked into the plane, as before.

"What time does your plane leave?"

"Three-thirty. Do we have time for lunch out?"

It was eleven a.m. The airport was only fifteen minutes away, but it would take time to check in and go through Customs. She had to declare the record, and she was petrified. Pyotr had briefed her. She should tell them it was an X-ray of her grandfather's cousin who fell off a bicycle. "They won't make you open it," he assured her.

"Do we have time for something quick in town?" she asked.

Pyotr looked at her funny. Maybe he was just realizing she was leaving the country, and maybe him, forever. "I want for you to have plenty of time. If we leave now, we'll be in good shape. Let's do the café with the great blintzes, yes?"

A great note to end on. Becka agreed.

After lunch, they headed to the airport. Pyotr told her how much he loved the music at the jam session. She was afraid the concertina came off sounding like a sick squirrel. He let out a snort and told her no, it created a beautiful shiny thread in the music. Just like her, he added.

When he parked outside the entrance to Pulkovo International and ran over to open Becka's door, she noticed a guy with a red beard leaning against a car across the street, glaring at Pyotr. Silvan Sloane. His swollen forearms looked ridiculous in comparison to his spindly little legs.

"Pyotr!"

He looked up and saw Sloane. With no hint of a smile on his face, he told her, "One moment, I promise."

Pyotr closed the door behind her and guided her to the icy sidewalk. He pointed his chin at the benches outside the big walkway into the airport. "Take a seat. I'll be right back."

Becka froze in place. She considered videoing whatever was about to happen. Pyotr stood straight and crossed the street.

Sloane started yelling at him. Pyotr widened his stance and Sloane called him something she couldn't make out. Then she clearly heard Pyotr.

"As I told you, *gandon*, I will have it for you next week." His right hand was starting to form into a fist. "We have worked together for many years. Give me the time I need and don't come looking for me again, *suka!*"

Sloane glanced over at Becka and saw that she was recording it on her phone. He growled something at

Pyotr and got back into his car, and, revving the engine for good measure, pulled away.

Pyotr came back and didn't look overly concerned. "Please put your phone away," he implored, a smile playing on his lips.

"What was that? Are you going to be okay? Maybe we should call the police."

A hearty laugh followed, but this time he grabbed her and gave her a bear hug.

"Nope, nyet, never. Don't you worry your beautiful self about it. He's all talk and no action. Besides, I am going to pay him next week."

Her only choice was to believe him and drop the conversation.

"What did you call him?" Becka asked, knowing it would at least be entertaining.

"Those curse words? They are actually much worse in English. One is, um, kind of like 'condom,' and the other is 'bitch,' but I suggest you do not use them, at least not here and not in Little Odessa, yes?"

"I won't."

He leaned in and whispered, "I trust you to delete that video, please. I will adore you for it."

She blew him a kiss.

She didn't say yes.

Pyotr had seconds to say a proper goodbye or they would send a police officer over to ticket him.

He stood by her on the sidewalk. People ran past them from all directions, trying to make planes, get home, start or end their vacations, and move on with their lives. Becka briefly considered staying and starting over in Russia, which of course was out of the question. This would just turn into a fantasy she summoned in her lonely hours, wondering *what if*. She had a job and a life near the ocean to get back to. It was time.

She was suddenly struck by how handsome he was. Long, dark hair, lashes that any woman would die for, broad shoulders and solid biceps. Jeans that hugged him in all the right places. Smelled like heaven and had a sexy accent, at least to a New Yorker.

"Come here, my little cream puff."

She would miss that.

He put his arms around her with a tightness that meant he'd caught some feelings for her. Then he put his face up to hers and kissed her so gently that she thought she would cry. He closed his eyes and savored a moment frozen in time. Becka loosened her grip on the luggage. It could easily fall away, vaporize and take the Dinah Shore bone record with it. Right then, none of those things mattered.

Becka wanted to stay there, Pyotr's lips brushing hers, his body warm and tight against her.

A tapping sound came from behind them. An officer with what looked like a pool cue rapped three times on the hood of the car and he glared at the back of Pyotr's head. When Pyotr pulled away from Becka, he nodded at the officer, who turned and left. It wasn't the first time he saw an infatuated American woman saying goodbye.

With her backpack on, the suitcase handle cutting into her right hand and the concertina case in her left, it was time to catch the plane. Or, rather, to lug herself into Customs, do the whole ridiculously long process, then board the first of three planes. It was going to be a tiresome journey.

Pyotr got back in his jalopy and blew her a kiss. Then he mouthed the words "I love you."

She caught his kiss in midair and mouthed the same thing back. Her eyes watered.

She walked into the airport, leaving him—possibly—forever.

Pulkovo International was packed. Becka was brusquely pushed forward and tumbled into a wall. Luckily, the cardboard tube protecting the bone record was nestled deep in her backpack.

Pyotr had written the word “Customs” in Russian and told her to look for the sign. She could hardly wait to walk through the blistering coals of language issues and guaranteed misunderstandings. There was no other way to get home unless her boyfriend owned a private jet that he didn’t tell her about. He was long gone, anyway; the gendarme with the long stick saw to that.

With a bladder that had started to throb, she rolled her way into a bathroom. It was spotless. She was nearly blinded by the fluorescents. On the way out of the stall, she caught a glimpse of a woman with crazy hair and stress lining her face. It was Becka. *You better calm down, sister*, she admonished herself. *Be smooth. Think about Winston cigarettes and blintzes.* But the thought of carrying a formerly bootlegged item hitching a ride between her shoulders sent an icicle of panic up her spine. *What if they pull me off the line and question me? What if they arrest me?*

Her therapist (the one she had terminated, so in actuality, she had none) would have called this catastrophizing. Becka smacked some cold water onto her face and patted it dry. She realized she needed to do something about her jaw. Unclenching it would help.

Pyotr was a genius in writing out a few Russian terms for her. He'd also printed out pictures of the different uniforms she might come across at the airport, from the Customs agents to the Moscow police (aka *militisya*) and the Federal Security Service ("FSB"). She did, in fact, have a translation guide in case Pyotr's suggestions were not enough. She felt as prepared as any mono-lingual American woman carrying an expensive piece of contraband could feel. *For Chrissakes, it's only Dinah Shore,* she mused. She inwardly apologized to Dinah Shore, who was a very accomplished musician who did a lot to break the glass ceiling for women and also color barriers.

But there was one other thing Pyotr said that was a "wild card." Although ninety-nine percent of bags were not searched, any of the personnel could, for no apparent reason, call you over and conduct a full-body, tear-open-your-bags search. Whoever stood out to them could warrant this special treatment, no explanations given.

"Do I look like somebody they would single out?" Becka had asked him.

"Not typically, but you have a way of looking people in the eye when you come across them. It must be a New York City thing."

"So don't do that?"

"Correct," he'd said. "A direct stare is a challenge. Look busy but not upset. Be happy, but don't smile. It's your best defense."

Could she remember all that? And how what if she was pulled aside?

He assured her that was extremely unlikely, but if it happened, she needed to keep her cool, answer their questions as generally as possible and not, under any circumstances, get uppity.

Then she thought of something worse, a catastrophe of another sort. She hadn't yet paid for the record. If Sofia was suddenly spooked by their recent encounter, she could alert authorities that the Dinah Shore was actually stolen.

Oh God, she thought, *why did I have to buy this damn record!*

Becka put her fertile imagination on hold. She glanced at the paper with the letters that meant Customs, took a deep breath, and rolled to the other end of a very long hall.

Forget TSA Pre-Check or anything resembling a shortcut. She had to lug everything onto the conveyer belt, empty her pockets (which held a Dramamine, an Excedrin and an Alka-Seltzer—the neurotic's Holy Trinity) and was ordered (with gestures) to take off her boots and socks. While she was being wanded and ogled, a guy in a pine-green uniform with an emblem of a two-headed phoenix in bright yellow flames put up his hand. A sister officer came over bearing Becka's backpack, which was completely split open at the zipper for all the world to see. She'd kept extra underwear in there, which by this point, had been used. The officer curtly waved Becka over to the table past the conveyor belt.

To her horror, Becka noticed that somehow, Silvan Sloane was now behind her on line and was about to walk through the metal detector.

With her heart battering against her ribcage, Becka turned back to the female officer who was now guiding her by the elbow to an area a few feet away.

"What is?" she demanded in English, looking at the instrument case. "Open."

Oh my God! They didn't care about the bone record, they were hung up on Athena. She broke out in the biggest smile they'd ever seen, at least on an American citizen.

"May I?" Becka asked, hoping she knew enough English to get it.

"*Plees.*"

Becka took it out and began to play the Russian anthem. Thank God Pyotr taught it to her. A warm look came over the officer's face. Her partner started mouthing the words, then nodded and motioned for her to pack up and get out of there.

Sloane didn't fare as well. After Becka shoved Athena back into the case and pushed her undies to the bottom of the backpack, she scrambled to her gate. She turned around for a second, only to see Silvan Sloane glaring at her, arms outstretched, being searched. She prayed his final destination wasn't Brighton Beach.

Being back home was a hard adjustment for Becka. While she reluctantly shook herself free of the glow of being with Pyotr, the anxiety of what she'd gone through with the bone record nagged at her.

After Monday's acclimation back to the hospital via a long, boring staff meeting, for the rest of the week she took the subway to two hospitals in Queens to calibrate their MRI machines.

Becka filed a new article with one of her professional journals and gave two online tutoring lessons. Keeping busy was the best way to ward off the shadow of Silvan Sloane, whose whereabouts were a mystery.

She already knew she was going to part with her bone record. In her mind, it was a done deal. The sooner she could ship it off somewhere—to Sofia, to Pyotr, or even Sloane if that kept him off her back—the better. As soon as the weekend came, she'd mail it wherever it needed to be to end this chapter in her life.

Before she knew it, she was typing "bone records" into Google. This was a huge mistake. Apparently, some news had broken while she was away that was of particular interest. The story was about to get worse.

US mystery writer assaulted during sightseeing tour in Paris; says culprit fled and stole her 'X-ray record,' made during the US-Soviet Union Cold War

She was on her lunch break when she read it and it stole her breath away. Of course, she had to read further.

"Cozy mystery writer Linda Gould says that it's been her dream to visit Paris. She'd heard about the recent rise in crime there, but coming from New York City, she knew how to travel safely. 'This man passed by me extremely fast and sliced open my backpack. I didn't have my wallet in it, but I forgot that I had something much more valuable.' Ms. Gould collects 'bone records,' bootleg jazz recordings from Russia made during the Cold War when Russian music lovers were prohibited from accessing American culture. The man who slashed her bag, she says, was over six feet tall and had 'mutton chop' sideburns and a red beard."

Becka froze. This Silvan Sloane guy, if that was really even his name, was deadly serious. *There's your sign,* she thought. *Time to bail. He can have my goddamned record.*

She needed to talk to Pyotr as soon as she got home from work. Against her better judgment, she would ask him for the best way to contact the hairy creep and get him off her case once and for all.

She scrolled down the page to read more news on the topic. Something terrifying caught her eye.

"Sequined smooth jazz musician's last purchase: a bone record from the USSR. Officials investigating for possible links to cause of death."

This was starting to sound much more like a murder than an accident. Sofia definitely mentioned Jerry Z had purchased the record, and somehow, he flew off the Verrazano Bridge.

Linda Gould was attacked in broad daylight.

Am I next?

♪

"Your Song" by Elton John started playing on Becka's phone.

Crap! I thought I blocked Jeff Wright.

"What?"

"Well, hello to you, too."

"Hey, Jeff, I almost didn't pick up. This better be good." She heard him take in a huge gulp of air.

"Becka...I'm really sorry for how things ended. For all the calls I got from those women I work with. I was such a jerk. I didn't really give us a chance, and I want to apologize for that."

"This isn't happening," she said, finger poised over the end call button.

"No, I'm not trying to get back together. Although, you know, I wouldn't balk at it."

"Jeff, get to the point. And no, we are most definitely not getting back together. I have *so* moved on."

That stung. "I'll get straight to it, then. The stuff that just happened to that smooth jazz musician you liked, the one who died or was killed. You were going to take your mother to see him?"

"So?"

Becka could hear him breathe. He obviously still had a thing for her. As pissed off as she was, the sound of her voice was like music to his ears. Why didn't he ever show her how he felt?

"I was worried about you, that's all. You said you were going over there to get a bone record, and the news mentioned that he was a fanatic about those things. I didn't know his real name was *Jerzy*...?"

Since the news had hit about the musician's death, Becka had wondered if their paths were somehow related, even if tangentially. It was like an Escher painting, all inverted staircases and impossible geometry. Was there a tie-in to any of this with Silvan Sloane, and the bigger question: Should she be worried?

She cleared her throat, determined to end the call as soon as possible. "I have no idea why he was killed. Maybe a 'me too' thing. He wasn't known to treat women so well. Maybe his Eastern European supplier of whatever—God knows—killed him. Maybe his neighbors did! Who cares!"

The stillness that followed lasted too long. He'd made his point, she wasn't interested, and there was nothing more to say.

"Okay, Becka. You have every reason to be upset with me. I wasn't that good of a boyfriend. I was just...worried about you." And then, because curiosity got the better of him and because he wasn't good with boundaries, he asked, "Did you end up getting one of those records too? Because that would be cool."

He was the one who gave me a hard time about going to Russia! Now it's 'cool' and he wants to know all about it?

"Yeah, I bought one. You wouldn't believe the things I did in ten days." She was mostly thinking about Pyotr. "But Jeff, do me a big favor."

"What is it?"

"Don't call me anymore."

The discussion reminded her of what lay ahead. Better to face things now than later, when God knew what Silvan Sloane would decide to do.

Since she got back from St. Petersburg, Becka hadn't heard word one from Lizzy. She didn't return any of Becka's calls or texts. Their friendship felt like twine. Little by little, it had quietly unraveled until one day, all the strands had pulled apart.

Becka was in a weird little bubble over in Russia. It felt refreshing to be so insulated from the news, able to temporarily ignore the post-election headlines. Moscow was in the news more and more, but visiting for ten days didn't seem like a risk. Or maybe her head was in the sand.

When Becka first got off the plane in St. Petersburg, she shot Lizzy a quick text. A few more texts followed just to stop her from worrying (*Pyotr is HOT!* and *Going to buy the you-know-what record!*). But Lizzy was silent. Did she not approve of the hookup? Funny; Lizzy's life was an amalgam of failed relationships brought on by her control freak tendencies. She had zero tolerance for anybody who deviated from her politics, her preferences in food or music, or anything else. The fact that she still counted Becka as a friend going on four decades was a puzzle.

Maybe she just kept Becka around for the sake of sentimentality. They grew up together, sharing innocent and not-so-innocent adventures, and navigated in and out of love affairs, jobs, deaths and disappointments. A common timeline didn't guarantee there was a viable and salvageable friendship anymore, though. Endurance without substance was meaningless.

The whole mess with Silvan Sloane was terrifying. Becka needed to resolve the situation immediately. She could really use a friend right about now.

Lizzy!....anybody home?

Crickets.

Come on, I need you. Where are you?

More crickets. Then: *I really don't have much to say to you.*

Becka let out an expletive and stared at her phone.

Lizzy, what the hell is going on?

If you must know, I'm opposed to your support of Russia at a time like this.

WTH? I'm calling you.

I won't answer.

Then what IS IT?? Tell me or I'm gonna call.

By going over there, you're showing support. I can't believe you don't see it.

This was craziness. Becka had no idea what drugs her friend had been taking but they weren't the good kind.

SUPPORT? I took American Airlines to Helsinki and then I had to fly to another crappy city before I landed in St. P. Over seventeen hours each way! And I seriously doubt my pocketful of rubles is going to bolster an economy that may or MAY NOT have meddled in the election.

Where was this coming from? Enough was enough. Becka tapped the phone icon.

“I told you not to call me.” Lizzy’s voice was crisp and dry.

“Yet here you are, picking up,” Becka spat. “What the hell is going on with you? I don’t even get how you’re offended here. Going to Russia was a problem?”

She could hear Lizzy take a sip of something. She’d been a teetotaler for more than ten years, ever since she veered off into the side of the Brooklyn Battery Tunnel and nearly spun around. Thank God nobody else was driving through it at the time. She was able to right herself and, as she exited the tunnel, pulled off on a side street in Lower Manhattan to catch her breath. It then became obvious that genetics did not predispose her to handle alcohol well.

“I already told you. You show poor support for your country.”

Becka’s mouth went sour. “It’s called *travel*, Lizzy. Listen, I don’t know what the hell your deal is lately, but your virtue signaling is really disrespectful to me.”

“Well, I was disrespected too.”

As she pulled the phone away from her ear, Becka thought she would give it one more try. This relationship, whatever it had become, was obviously at death’s door.

“I’ll bite. How exactly were you disrespected?”

A few beats later, after what sounded like a big gulp of something on the other line, Lizzy came back to earth. “Sohrab went back home.”

So it definitely wasn’t Becka “daring” to travel to Russia. It was a boyfriend issue. Even more puzzling, because why had Lizzy taken it out on Becka? That made no kind of sense.

"Lizzy, are you...drinking?"

"It's none of your fucken business, but yes."

Sohrab, who was from Iran, was brilliant, fascinating and more handsome than anybody had a right to be. He adored Lizzy and, as far as Becka could tell, treated her very well. He was kind to Lizzy's two kids. The family had been through a difficult divorce and Sohrab caught some hate from the kids, but eventually, they welcomed him into their lives.

According to Lizzy, her boyfriend was homesick. But the more Lizzy talked (Becka caught the hint of a slur), the more it seemed that something had happened to put the relationship on ice.

"I mean, he could have been missing his family." Not wanting to come off as harsh, Becka added, softly this time, "Maybe you two weren't a good fit."

Becka had so much on her mind without having to worry about her relationship with Lizzy. She was terrified of Sloane coming after her and really wanted to tell Lizzy about it. Lizzy would know how to calm her down and help her deal with it. Those days seemed to be over.

And now Lizzy was off to the races, talking more expansively than before. "Wha did you want to talk to me about...Peeeeter?"

Thank God Lizzy was at home, safe. She'd fall out soon, Becka thought. Tomorrow was another day, and she could start to deal with her drinking again.

Hopefully, she'd get the help she needed and find her way back to sobriety.

"It's really nothing. Hey, where are the kids?"

"They're wi' Steeeve."

Becka shut her eyes and spoke. "Do you need me to come over?" She desperately hoped Lizzy would say no, but she'd drive there if she had to.

"Nope. Gu nite."

Lizzy had dealt with her addiction years ago in therapy and AA. Strangely, even though they were so close, she had never told Becka about it. But don't best friends talk about their demons?

I'll check in with her tomorrow unless she still wants to crap on our friendship.

There was only one other person who could help her deal with Sloane.

Way up in a much higher latitude, Pyotr was doing his own thinking about somebody special.

Talk tonite? Your tonite? A heart emoji followed.

You betcha. I miss being called a breakfast food.

Okay, my little waffle. Zoom with me at your 9p.

We can virtual-cuddle. Catch you then.

Becka's nine was Pyotr's four a.m. *He would do that for me!* She smiled and pictured him on the bed; on her laptop, which would be on her bed.

Maybe having a whirlwind romance far from home scratched a certain itch she'd had since breaking it off with Jeff. And she definitely didn't want to go back to the Jeffs of the world, the discarded, damaged or divorced; not that she was a big draw, either. Never married, stubborn and unwilling to put up with somebody in the same house for more than two or three days tops. She was not a good candidate for a long-term relationship, but she did enjoy the falling in love part.

Pyotr so was different from Jeff. Not just his background and his tastes and the way he viewed life, but also because he appreciated Becka's independence and desire for a lot of space. Most of the women she knew, even her friends (especially Lizzy), liked to breathe the same air as their boyfriends and husbands. They intertwined every facet of their lives with their significant others. Only the scraps were left.

Constantly being in each other's space would give her anxiety attacks. She knew it from the one time she'd stayed over at Jeff's house and gone to work from there the next morning, then came back later for dinner with him and Cody and stayed over again. It was too damn much togetherness. To say nothing of being confusing for his son, which she now regretted. At least they didn't fight that week; they saved that nonsense for the months that followed. And boy, were they big fights. It hardly mattered now what they were about. Jeff was a dot on a timeline.

To be honest, as different as he was from Jeff, she knew Pyotr wouldn't be a great fit either. He lived a hidden life that wasn't suited to an honest relationship, starting off with the fact that she had no idea what he really did for a living. Toward the end of her visit, she'd seen him screaming into the phone, cheeks nearly purple, when he was dealing with "clients." He told her very little about them, and she was one hundred percent sure she didn't want to know.

They'd only been together for a few magical days, without the need to work out their finances, decide who made the bed and who made the coffee, or why the cap from the toothpaste was always missing. It was fantasy. All they had to do for the better part of ten days was to drink each other in, play house, eat some exquisite meals, and that was it. Absolutely nothing to realistically base a relationship on.

Still, as Becka looked down from her eerily quiet apartment to the street eleven floors below, observing the arteries of traffic in and out of southeastern Brooklyn, she wondered about all the humanity encased in just her building alone. Did all of them—did any of them—have love in their lives? Did they dream up their own definition of "perfect" and then go for it?

By three in the afternoon, both bundles of clothes were done, thanks to the leftover detergent pods in the kitchen drawer. There were a few hours of daylight left, and the December winds would pick up soon. If Becka hankered for a walk on the beach, now was the time. All she wanted was a quick stroll with a steaming cup of tea from the corner Greek diner and a hearty onion knish from Mrs. Kahn's, followed by a bedtime "discussion" with Pyotr...and after that, she promised herself she'd put this chapter behind her and return to reality.

For tonight's Zoom, she'd chosen some sultry music from Vanji, found a revealing satin pajama top and dusted off a sage-scented candle.

But there would be no moonlit pillow talk. What Pyotr was about to tell her would ruin any shred of the seductive fantasy evening she planned on.

"What did you just text me about Silvan Sloane?" Becka's eyes were wide and her breathing was choppy. Right before the Zoom, he'd sent two lines that ran her blood cold.

"Hello, my sweet," he purred.

"Pyotr, what the hell is going on? Why did you say Sloane was 'going to be trouble'?"

Pyotr sighed, glanced appreciatively at her outfit, and realized this wasn't going to be any kind of romantic reunion.

Whenever he was being serious, his smile drooped to a straight line. "So right after you saw him at the airport, he actually texted me. He knew you were going to report back to me."

"*Report back*? This creeper is at the same airport I'm at, and I tell you that I'm absolutely freaking out, and now this is a *news story* I'm writing? I have to *report back*?" She couldn't stop her chest from rising and falling in staccato beats.

"Please, calm down."

Becka glared at him.

"He said he was on his way to Paris to look at bone records. The reason he made eye contact with you was to ask if he could buy your Dinah Shore record before you got to your gate."

"You told him my gate?!" Becka pulled up her neckline.

"No, of course not! But then Customs yanked him off the line. He had a few rare films hidden in a big book that they confiscated."

"Poor Silvan, like I care. What 'trouble' do you mean? I'm starting to lose my shit here. Just tell me!"

This conversation was long past saving. Flirting was off the table. Suddenly he became just somebody she'd spent a few days with.

"I believe he wants to make you a good offer for the Dinah record."

"Perfect. I can't wait to get rid of this thing. But not through him. I'm going to send it back where it came from. Let him chase it from there."

"Okay, Becka, the reason I'm calling it a problem is that...he has a way of being heavy-handed."

"From making an offer to threatening me for it? Forget it! I'm going to call the police." Becka could feel her pulse striking like a drum roll.

Pyotr tried a smile. It wasn't convincing.

"I'm sorry," he said. "All I wanted to tell you is that he may try to contact you on your socials and ask you about, uh, parting with it. If I were you, I'd say yes."

The prospect of this crook contacting her directly was terrifying. Becka tasted bile and swallowed it back down.

She couldn't believe she'd been in the same room as this demon blithely playing "I Remember You" on her accordion with her new Russian buddies. It also started to occur to her that maybe it was Sofia who told him about her.

"And damn Sofia, too! I thought she was cool. I thought it was just a normal transaction."

Now Pyotr's smile was wider and more relaxed. He crinkled his eyes. Becka resisted with difficulty. She really had better plans for this conversation.

"Honey, nothing is a 'normal transaction' with bootlegs. Even seventy-year-old scraps of X-ray film that only five people in the world care about."

She couldn't bear the thought of calling the police and decided to sleep on everything, figure it out in the morning.

"I paid her for it already, so it looks like I'm going to be out the seven-fifty if I send it back or, the way it's looking now, *giving* it to Silvan. That really burns me up, I gotta tell you."

"Well...maybe there's a way you can keep it."

"No, forget it. I need to have a clean slate with Sofia. I don't want anybody else coming after me. I can't believe I'm asking you this, but how do I get it to him?"

Pyotr had already anticipated this question. "Let Sloane contact you. You can ship it to him and be done with it. The money—"

"I know. I wrote it off already." Becka started calculating how to absorb the loss. Better to be rid of that slimeball than to worry about a third of her rent. A dead tenant owes no rent, anyway.

Pyotr tried a smile. "What I wanted to say is that I feel responsible. I brought you into this, although I didn't think he'd be such a *suka*."

Stretching her neck from side to side helped reset her emotions. "Okay. I have a better idea. I'm just gonna send it back to Sofia, and she can deal with him. Let him come after her. What a fucking bully, though."

"Welcome to my world."

"Why didn't you warn me?"

"Look. This guy has a ton of these records. He got some from Ukraine, some from an album collector in Los Angeles, and one in Paris after he mugged that lady. There was a character in the UK who'd written a book about it and he had a few records too. Silvan strong-armed him, in broad daylight, if you can believe it."

"Of course I can. How did that go?"

"Let's just say he got what he came for."

Becka's mouth was desiccated. She was ready to put this behind her. But there was one last question she had to ask.

"Will he go away when he gets the record?"

"Definitely. There's nothing else he wants from you but to own a full collection. He wants to own all of them."

"He sure doesn't look like a jazz lover."

"Correct. He's only in it for the resale value," Pyotr told her. "He couldn't give one shit about the music. At some point, he'll sell the whole kite and caboodle."

"Kit." A laugh fell out of her that she didn't intend.

Pyotr's chocolate brown eyes drifted to the ribbon at the edge of her pajama top. "Is that ribbon pink or red? Can I maybe get a closer look?"

Becka was chewing on a chocolate croissant at her desk, flipping through Brooklyn Live Magazine. She'd clocked in her usual twenty minutes early. Strangely, even though her recent Russian getaway would be forever memorable, she had missed her office while she was away. There was something comforting about her own space, being able to work at her desk while listening to music on YouTube. Today she was feeling wistful about the whole Jerry Zolotov situation. She found his concert from 1997 and put it on in the background.

She was back to real-world tasks, which meant contacting the radiology heads of the hospitals in her territory and finding out what issues they were having. Based on their feedback, she'd set up an itinerary that would take two months to get through. At each site, she'd be responsible for troubleshooting equipment issues, making calibrations on old machines when it was possible to do so, and when it wasn't, identifying parts that needed to be ordered to repair them. Then she'd sweep through the area again to install the new parts.

Her territory included the township where Jeff Wright lived. She wondered how Cody was doing and felt a momentary pang of something for Jeff. Not fondness or longing, but missing the familiar terrain of a "normal" relationship. Things with Pyotr were so complicated and out there; Becka was afraid to admit to herself, against everything she knew to be rational, that she still wanted to be with him. A slip of the tongue was all it took to cement her decision about her Russian lover once and for all.

Just about the last thing she needed was a cryptic email, especially at work.

The name Linda Gould in the "from" was vaguely familiar. Normally, something like this would feel like spam, but something made her leave it in her inbox.

She thought about the call the night before with Pyotr. How she wanted—needed—to be done with this chapter, even though getting over him was turning out to be one of the hardest things she ever had to do. The way a lock of hair fell in his eyes, the way his mouth twisted when he was about to laugh. He was sexy and perceptive and so much more.

Ten minutes later, the phone buzzed again. A new email. The subject was "Linda Gould/Bones."

Who on earth was "Linda Gould" and why was she writing to Becka twice?

She had a bad feeling about it with the mention of "bones." The right thing to do would have been to wait until she got home to read it.

She hadn't done the right thing since she started carrying on with a man halfway around the world.

The first email read:

Dear Ms. Becka Rifkin,

You may have heard of me LOL! I'm an author (of mysteries) and also a jazz fanatic. I used to play the tuba, if you can believe that, in college marching band.

Anyway, I've become a collector of music ephemera. It inspires me to write my novels, which are called "cozy mysteries." Usually, the heroine has to figure out a whodunit by following musical clues. I would say these are on the light side and almost quaint at times. I'm deep into my second series.

That's why I'm writing to you. I can't find anybody else on the East Coast who has a bone record. I don't know if you heard, but I was attacked in Paris by a man who stole my bone record. It was in the news. It was so embarrassing, but then I thought who knows, maybe it'll help sell a few books!

I am prepared to make an offer to buy this from you. I happen to love Dinah Shore, too. My new work-in-progress is a mystery about a singer and I would love to use her as my inspiration!

Becka's heart froze in her throat. How could a stranger have found out about this? She was afraid to read more. She put the phone on her desk and walked away to open a file cabinet, then closed it back up and went back to her desk.

Linda Gould continued:

I hope this doesn't alarm you, but I'm in an online group that specializes in jazz collectibles and somebody, I forgot who, mentioned that you had one of these bone records. I sure hope I have the right Becka Rifkin!

Do you think I can listen to it as soon as possible? We can do a Zoom call and you can play it for me! Like I said, I'd love to buy it from you if by some chance you want to sell it.

Please respond ASAP. My heroine is counting on me!

Warmest regards,
Linda Gould

The second email was obviously an attempt to come off as friendly. Becka didn't know what to make of it.

PS - I really hope I didn't scare you. Authors are a tenacious lot, but not to worry! I only want it for inspirational reasons! -- LG

Normally, Becka wouldn't give two hoots about this author or her "cozy mysteries," but coupled with the Silvan Sloane situation, her paranoia was now out of control.

It's hard to get over somebody who's been part of your life since you were a kid. Becka still missed Lizzy and cried for a week until she was emptied of all emotion.

The following week, she'd be traveling to Connecticut to work on the MRI machines at a few of the different standalone sites Shore Unity owned.

The hospital was in a high tax bracket neighborhood with mature, towering sycamores overlooking well-kept Tudor homes. It reminded her of where Lizzy lived.

Becka started to think about all the shapes that finally, at middle age, fit together so snugly. Now Lizzy had gone and yanked one out, and the whole sorry structure was collapsing.

That Friday, gearing up for her last day in Connecticut, Becka received a text from Lizzy.

I'm ok but we're not. I have to leave this behind.

Becka was in the hospital parking lot, waiting to clock in and finish her reports for the week. She sat in her car and smacked the dashboard.

What r u talking about!?

I just can't.

Not a great way to start the day, Becka thought. As much as she wanted to avoid a fight, she had to know what was going on, but quickly. In seven minutes, she'd have to put on her work face.

She pressed the call icon.

"Lizzy, what the hell is your problem?"

"Really?!" Her voice was raspy. It didn't sound like Lizzy at all. Not slurred, not angry, just ghost-like.

"Yeah, really! What did I do to you, or what do you *think* I did to you?"

"I can't believe you voted for that senile sociopath! Then you go to *Russia*—"

"Wait. What? Since when do politics...."

A double beep came through. Lizzy was getting another call. What could be more important than dealing with this right now?

"I have someone on the other line," Lizzy mumbled. I gotta go."

With nothing resolved, the whole friendship was in the lurch, or maybe just over for good.

The next day, Becka gave things one last try. It was a Saturday and she was going to make her very last call to Lizzy.

After three rings, a recording kicked in. "This customer is not available. Goodbye." Was it her imagination or did the robotic voice put a slight punch on the "bye"?

Things weren't looking good.

Music had saved her soul more than once. She smiled as she remembered the night with the musicians at the dry cleaners. She needed to look around for a local music scene that didn't scoff at the accordion. Little Athena hadn't seen any action since Russia. Maybe she also felt like a neglected friend.

She walked along the piers and stopped in front of a diner. Brooklyn was famous for its gleaming eateries with bloated cakes in the window. Hunger kicked in. A fluffy veggie omelet with a slice of toasted challah sounded like God's answer to loneliness.

Just outside the diner was a splintered telephone pole festooned with flyers of all kinds: missing dogs, moving-out sales, part-time jobs and a yellow flyer bleached by the sun with the words: "Small community band seeks musicians. All instruments welcome. We play for fun, not profit!" She snapped a photo. Maybe her next best friend was waiting to meet her.

"Check your Insta."

It had been a week since she last heard from Pyotr and she was adjusting to not having him around to talk to. Pyotr's text sounded ominous.

They arranged a call and he looked yummy, as usual. She felt a familiar warmth on her face. Who wants to waste time discussing social media when they could be gazing at this hot specimen of a man?

"Hey, hun! You look great."

"Mmm. You too!"

"So what's this about my Instagram? I'm on it now."

"Your new follower. See it?"

She checked; she did have a new follower, but how would Pyotr know that? And why was he looking at her account anyway?

"Okay, I see a new account on here. 'SovJazz.' Let me click on that."

"I'll wait."

Becka's jaw dropped. There were images of jazz artists playing all kinds of instruments, album covers and some videos. Then she saw SovJazz's latest post—of a bone record. The caption: *Dinna Shore.* Even worse, he tagged her:

Come out, come out, wherever you are, Miss Becka!

"Holy crap! Why is this psychopath posting about the record I bought? And why is he tagging ME?"

"I need to tell you something."

She ignored him. “Well, I’m just gonna block him.”

“Don’t do that.”

“Why not?”

“That little message was just the beginning. He’ll just never give up, Becka. He wants that record.”

“I can see that!” She nearly threw her phone across the room. Now maybe it was time to call the police.

“Calm down,” he said. “Let me talk you through this.”

“Talk fast. I’m about to throw up.”

Her boyfriend’s chest hair peeked out from his half-buttoned shirt. She couldn’t care less.

“Look, Silvan’s a creep, but he’s really harmless. He knows Sofia. They’re business associates. He got most of his X-rays from her and he makes a lot of money on them. If I know anything about him, he can *treeple* what you paid to Sofia.”

Becka went silent.

“You did pay her, yes? Don’t make a fool out of me. A lovesick guy, okay. But not a fool.”

“I told you I did! But damn, this thing is a hot potato.”

“Thank you for paying, my little waffle.”

No reaction. Not even a smile.

“I think you should respond,” he said. “But it’s up to you.”

“No! I saw how you almost got into a fistfight with him at the dry cleaners. He’s out of his mind, and he’s violent! I’m not touching this!”

Pyotr looked at her kindly. “That’s up to you, but you that ‘misunderstanding’ on the street was really about you," he said. "I didn't want to tell you and freak you out."

"Holy shit! I'm sure freaking out now, Pyotr. Just tell me what to do!"

"Ship it back to me or to Sofia. That should take care of things. He'll find out that it's out of your hands, and then he can buy it from one of us and be done with it."

"Was he really trying to rob you out on the street? Or rather, rob me?" Becka couldn't believe how this was unfolding. She wished she'd never even heard of bone records.

"No. When you saw us talking, he was offering a much higher price than what you paid. But I could see how happy you were to have the record, and I wasn't gonna let anyone take that away from you."

"I appreciate that, but I'm still not clear about the airport. And then seeing him being pulled aside by Customs. What was that all about?"

"He was on a business trip." Air quotes followed. "When he got to the airport, they stopped him. He had four different bone records wrapped up in wax paper inside an Ansel Adams photography book. You know who he is?"

"Of course," she said. "I'm surprised you do."

He shook his head. That stung.

"Anyway, the pages of the book were blank. The *politsiya* noticed right away."

It was a dummy book to hide his records in. According to Sofia, it had worked for him before, but as Sloane's luck would have it, one of the officers was a photography buff; Ansel, he knew, didn't take blank shots.

"After about two hours, they let him go with the records, which was unusual. Normally, in a case like this, they would just confiscate something like that. By that time, he missed his plane to Paris, which was his destination. So he wasn't following you. Not specifically."

"Yeah, I know." She remembered Linda Gould. "We both know who he was following. I mean, it was in the news."

She didn't tell him about being contacted by the mystery author. Maybe something bad would happen to her again. Who knew what Silvan Sloane would do next?

"So you're saying if I send it to you ASAP, I'm off the hook, right?"

"I believe so." That was all he had.

"Well then, I should never see him again. Right?"

The next day, when she got home from work, Becka decided to respond to Silvan Sloane's message on Instagram. There was no sense running anymore. She was tired of everything being so complicated and wanted him to be clear on where things stood with Dinah Shore: one, that she'd paid for the record, and two, that she was sending it back.

@sovjazz, I have paid in full for this. Why don't you check with Pyotr or Sofia, as I am shipping DINAH back to them the minute I can get to the post office!

Fuck him, she thought. Let him run around a little and try to find out where the damn thing was going to end up.

This had been a seven-hundred-fifty-dollar mistake. In essence, she was paying for the privilege of keeping it safe from a criminal (or "for" a criminal?) and then returning it to the original source (or someone close to her), who seemed to be in some kind of cahoots with Sloane, anyway. *A full circle...jerk.*

The Zoom calls were becoming tiresome, but Becka saw an end in sight. For the situation with Sloane and maybe, probably, with Pyotr.

He looked a little frazzled this evening. She forgot that the time difference was usually in her favor.

"I'm going to make a little side visit to Sloane and tell him to stop harassing you."

"I cannot tell you how much I'd appreciate that," she said, managing a wan smile. "But I reached out to him on Instagram. So he knows it's out of my hands. Literally."

Pyotr offered to pay for the record and the shipping himself.

She shook her head. "Why should you? This was all my dumbass mistake. Deciding to buy it in the first place."

Pyotr took a draw on his Winston. "The only dumbass mistake was for Sofia to tell Sloane about it. I understand why she did, but she could have just refused to tell him."

"At this point, it's whatever. This has been way more trouble than it's worth."

"Well, more so for Jerry Zolotov, eh? Thank God you only have Dinah Shore!"

Though he was trying to lighten the mood, he was right. The international effort to find Jerry's killer had heated up. Then something flew into Becka's mind and she blurted out, "Oh shit!"

"What is it?"

"It seems everyone connected with these stupid bone records is in jeopardy. That woman Linda Gould was roughed up, who, like I told you, emailed me, then Jerry was, well, whatever happened to him. Am I next in the line of fire? What if it wasn't Silvan who killed Zolotov and there's an even worse fruitcake looking for somebody who owns a bone record?" She felt the pulse in her temples.

Pyotr pounded the table. "I've decided! I'm paying for this and it will all go away."

"No, I won't let you."

He smiled and licked his lips. “I tell you what. I’ll put seven-fifty toward a plane ticket for you. We can meet in Paris if you like, when this is all over. In the summertime. Wouldn't that be nice?”

She was so deep in panic mode that she didn’t even catch the flirtatious direction he was trying to take the conversation.

“Okay,” she said after a long pause. “I owe you, and I don’t mean for the money, I mean for taking the heat off me. For dealing with Sofia and Sloane.”

“No need to. I just signed a new client and—”

“Not sure I need to know. Right?”

“Right. Sorry.”

“Take my advice,” he said. “When you go to the post office, insure it, get a receipt, then get a bottle of something smooth and red. Then call me.”

“Sounds like a plan. A good one.” Becka puffed out her cheeks and let the air seep out slowly. Then she frowned.

“What’s wrong?” Pyotr asked.

“I really think for my protection I should contact the police. Here where I live, not Interpol or anything.”

Pyotr hit the table again. This time, Becka jumped.

“What the hell!?” she yelped.

“Sorry, my sweet, but no. Where we are from, you don’t involve the police even if your throat is being sliced.”

“Nice imagery. But here, we do. Or maybe I’ll get a lawyer. I’m too tired to talk about this anymore. I need to go.”

Pyotr was looking forward to some lovey-dovey time but it wasn't going to happen. The next thing on his list was to contact Sloane and make sure he was going to leave Becka alone.

But there was one thing you knew about Silvan Sloane, if you knew anything at all. He didn't like being told what to do.

The post office didn't care much for Becka's cardboard packaging and slipped it inside a sturdier container. It would cost an extra ten bucks, but that didn't matter. The package would go on a very long journey. It wasn't expected to be delivered for at least five weeks.

"You can insure this and use the regular US Postal Service, but if it's one-of-a-kind, I highly suggest flying it out by DHL."

"Which has a better guarantee of actually getting to its destination?"

"You taking it there yourself." The guy smiled. "Seriously, it's been an issue lately with all this hubbub about the election. Nobody really knows how freight is going to be affected."

"Okay. Carrier pigeon, then. Just pick one and tell me what I owe you."

"They're both going to run you about thirty-five bucks. Then you'll want to insure it, right? What's the value?"

"Too much. Like $750." She winced. Delayed buyer's remorse.

"Okay, so DHL or PO?"

"DHL sounds good."

He did some quick calculations.

"Total with insurance is gonna be $44.12."

"Um, I'll come back."

"Excuse me?"

"Just not sure who I want to send it to. Or if I do."

The puffy clouds over the ocean glowed white. Becka breathed in the briny air and remembered what she loved about living at the edge of Brooklyn.

Somewhere in the ocean, Jerry Z was telling his tale of woe to the fish. For all anybody knew, maybe the smooth jazz man just wanted to go for a swim.

She'd just have to wait and find out what really happened when everybody else did. When the time came, it would be a shock to all.

“And don’t forget Becka Rifkin.” Officer Gloria Frost of the Sheepshead Bay precinct in southeastern Brooklyn sipped her green tea. She had a glistening French cruller on her desk that was begging to be eaten. The precinct was known for its overweight personnel, but not Frost. She watched what she ate and worked out five days a week. The cruller was a rare treat.

“Yeah. But she’ll probably end up being ruled out,” her partner Justin Kline said. “Since we got this case, there’s been slim pickings on the homicide.”

“If that’s what it is,” Frost noted. “Could have been a despondent musician, or maybe he was kidnapped.”

She confirmed it: the first bite of a New York City cruller was the most sublime.

“The break-in was called in by his head of security two days after Zolotov’s car was found on the Verrazano,” she continued. “Supposedly the muscle comes from Mossad. That thing that was stolen, well, you heard about it, right?”

“Yeah, some artwork?” Kline wanted a pastry too.

“Yes and no. The frame cost like thousands. It’s original artwork. But what’s in the frame cost over two mill.”

Kline whistled.

“A ‘bone record’ from Russia,” Frost told him. “I never heard of that before. Pretty esoteric, huh?”

"Let's get over to talk with that lady, Rebecca whatever, so we can cross her off our list," Kline said. "I have a feeling this case won't be going anywhere on our watch. It's heating up in Moscow and St. Petersburg, but Brooklyn, I'm not so sure about. Anyway, I'm positive that this woman has a squeaky-clean record."

"Well, Jay—"

"Eesh! My ex-wife called me that and I'm very much ready to forget her."

"Sorry, Justin. I mean, of course she's clean, but somebody knows something. There are too many secrets in Little Odessa. If there's anyone around these local clubs, or 'dance halls' as they call them, who knew Jerry Z, we might get a lead."

The saxophonist's death was almost three weeks old. Criminal Justice 101 said that for every day beyond the first week, the chances of catching a perp diminished dramatically, especially in an international situation like this one was shaping up to be. Open up this case to a place like Russia where the authorities wouldn't particularly care to collab with the FBI, and there were too many places for a perp to hide.

The strongest suspect was an operative who went by the name Silvan Sloane, which made the cops laugh. It was as un-Russian a name as you could possibly come up with. "Sounds like some billionaire villain in a romance novel to me," Gloria Frost had joked.

"We'll find out his real name, don't you worry," Kline assured her.

Sloane was identified as the prime suspect in the Linda Gould case. By assaulting the author in broad daylight at the Eiffel Tower in Paris (with more security cameras per square foot than the United Nations), it basically guaranteed his face was plastered everywhere, ensuring—the authorities hoped—a quick apprehension.

Sloane, whose actual record only consisted of one petty theft, had always managed to evade the law for his many alleged crimes. Not this time. When he was caught two days later a few miles from Paris, he was placed on bail, free to walk around, because the French tribunal court didn't see him as a flight risk. Naturally, the next day, he was already missing. Both Frost and Kline figured if he was coming to the States at all, it would be to their neck of the woods. Sheepshead Bay, Little Odessa, Manhattan Beach...and they'd be the ones catching the case.

The next morning was an all-day training session at Shore Unity Hospital. Becka enjoyed the walk from her apartment. It would give her a chance to think, get her fitness steps in and take the sea air into her lungs.

The hospital's eastern side had spectacular views of the Atlantic, and since the session was going to be in the main conference room on the fifth floor, she wanted to get there early to grab the best seat. Edison-Hayes was known to provide a nice spread for their training sessions: a warm breakfast and a catered lunch, not the tasteless wraps with a crabapple stuck in a flimsy paper box that most sessions had. Today they would be discussing new technologies coming down the pike and trying to sell their overpriced machines to the Shore Unity. Becka was excited to learn something cutting-edge. Always good for building the old résumé.

It felt good to think about work again. Three long blocks on Shore Parkway stood between her and the hospital. She took her puffy coat from the hall closet and blew a kiss to the portrait of her mother that Lizzy's artistic sister Nola had done. It was a beautiful treatment in watercolor. Just a glance brought back a good feeling about her mom. She let it seep in.

As she pushed the closet door closed, her doorbell sounded. This was highly unusual. Even the landlord would call first before showing up, unless there was an emergency.

One look out her peephole and her heart sank. There were two uniformed police officers in the little fisheye lens. She opened her door a crack. "Can I help you?"

"Officers Kline—K L I N E—and Frost here, ma'am." The taller one, a woman, showed her badge.

Becka opened the door all the way. Whatever this was about wasn't going to help her get a good seat in the conference room. *Here goes nothing.* "Yes, officers. How can I help you?"

"May we come in? I'm Officer Gloria Frost. This here is Officer Justin Kline."

"K-L-I-N-E, ma'am."

That was unnecessary, she thought.

Becka brought them about four feet into her living room. She lowered herself to the ottoman and gestured for them to use the couch. They remained standing, so Becka stood back up.

"What's this about?"

Officer Kline made a popping sound with his lips. He glanced around Becka's apartment. Sure didn't look like she had something to hide, especially a murder. She probably couldn't kill an ant on a kitchen counter.

"We're investigating the death of Jerry Zolotov. You're familiar with—"

"Yes." She almost added *unfortunately*, then realized that might raise an eyebrow.

"Just a few questions, then. Did you know him personally?"

Panic flushed through her body. Of course she didn't know him. But did she need a lawyer before she said anything? She made a split-second decision to cooperate. It wasn't because Office Kline had pale blue eyes, but that didn't hurt.

"No, I didn't. Just that he's, he was, a jazz musician and his body was found about three weeks ago."

"There is information that you purchased a 'bone record.' Is this true?"

Becka swallowed. In for a penny, in for a ruble, and now she was about to waive her rights to keep silent.

"Yes."

Gloria Frost watched Becka's face intently. The officer got a good feeling from this woman. Just another working stiff who had a thing for jazz. Nothing to see here. "Tell us how you acquired it."

That jolt again. Becka didn't know how much to tell. She decided to tell the truth, just maybe pull back a little.

"I visited a friend in Russia who knew I was into jazz and I was looking to get a bone record. Just to say I owned one. Maybe play it on my phonograph, I'm not sure."

"Who's it by?" asked K-L-I-N-E.

Who was this guy trying to kid? They probably already knew everything about it. She continued.

"Dinah Shore."

"That's my girl!" Frost chimed in. Then she caught the side-eye from her partner. "Sorry! Couldn't help it."

That seemed to lighten the mood.

"So when you bought it, was Jerry Zolotov mentioned at all?" Frost asked.

Hmm. Becka reconsidered how much these cops knew. They were skipping over some important stuff.

Hopefully I can get crossed off their list. Imagine me, a suspect.

“Yes. The woman who sold it to me said she sold him a record and then proceeded to inform me that he was just found near the Palisades, in the water.”

“Who did the song on that record, the one that was sold to Zolotov?” Frost asked.

“Who sang it, you mean?” Becka didn’t want to get into the whole thing about Stalin. No need to muddy the waters that played host to a dead body.

“Yes, who’s it by?”

“Well, it was ‘Polka Dots and Moonbeams’ by Sinatra. Also, if you know jazz, the Tommy Dorsey Orchestra.”

“No shit.” Officer Kline scribbled something on his pad. “Just taking a note for myself to listen to it. Sometimes things like this help me get into the right frame of mind to solve a case. Or at least put some of the pieces together.”

Becka was getting ready to wrap it up with a sigh when Officer Frost started back in.

“Ms. Rifkin, can you tell us the name of the person who sold the record to you?”

“All I know is her name is Sofia.”

“And have you ever heard of a Silvan Sloane?”

It felt like a boa constrictor had just grabbed her neck.

“Yes.”

“Tell us about him. Did you meet him?”

Becka felt for the edge of her kitchen chair behind her and decided to sit. This was going to take a while. She wouldn't get the best seat in the house or perhaps any seat. How late could she show up for training, anyway?

"Can I just text my boss that I'm delayed for...a few minutes?" Hopefully they'd get the hint.

Officer Frost nodded.

Kline jumped in. "Okay, so Sloane, huh? Doesn't sound Russki to me."

Ah. A real winner.

"Yes, so. My boy—my *friend* had an altercation with him. He told me that Sloane was upset about a job that he, my friend, was doing. I wasn't privy to the details. Then a few days later, when I was playing a jam session in a dry cleaners—"

"Is that where they typically perform music?" Kline cleared his throat, an attempt at a joke.

"No, but in this case, it was the first time I saw Sloane. He barged into the room we were playing in. It was very impromptu."

"What do you play?"

Was Kline interested or *interested*?

"Accordion. In this case, the concertina, because it's more portable."

"No shit."

What a varied and educated vocabulary.

"Anyway," she added, "he was also upset about something that, like I mentioned before, I wasn't told the details of. Later that night, my friend told me Sloane wanted a bone record. Not sure which one."

"Mmm hmm. Were you aware that he assaulted—allegedly assaulted—an author from the US who was on vacation in Paris?"

"I heard that, yes."

"So now, did you know Jerry? Did you ever meet him?"

Why are they repeating themselves?

"Again, no, but I followed his career somewhat. I was going to take my mother to see him, but she died before I got a chance to get it together." Becka's eyes watered.

Kline snapped his memo pad shut. "I don't think we have any more questions."

"If we need to dig deeper here, we can contact you?" Officer Frost had a warm smile. It didn't seem like she was trying to trip Becka up.

"Absolutely."

"Thank you for your time," Kline said. "Oh, and Miss Rifkin?"

"Yes?"

"Buddy Rich on drums and Bunny Berigan on trumpet in '*Polka Dots*.' Worth a listen."

Turned out she was only a half-hour late. Just as she anticipated, the training was chock-full of jargon and buzzwords with lots of ass-kissing in between. Edison-Hayes didn't disappoint in that regard. At least the lunch was good.

Seven hours later, the training was over. She'd have to sit through one more day of it. *That's tomorrow's headache,* she thought.

Becka walked along the fishing piers of Sheepshead Bay and watched the December sunset gain saturation. To say it felt like two days in one was an understatement.

She reached her high-rise. The elevator took forever to get to the lobby. Another tenant was waiting to take her dog upstairs after a run-in with another dog on Bay 28th Street, a Maltese that had the nerve to nip her dog in the back, which deposited some slime in the encounter.

"Did you call your vet?" Becka asked, reaching down to coo at the whippet.

"No, but I should have," the distraught owner replied. "The other dog didn't draw blood. The owner is a real jerk. I've run into him before, and he lets his dog off-lead before we open the gate to the dog park."

That was generous. It was more of a schoolyard with two city blocks' worth of dirt and a few sparse patches of grass hemmed in by ugly metal fencing.

"It's a joke. They have cameras too, but his guy just doesn't care. I'll have to walk over to the one on Bay 37."

Cameras.... It got Becka thinking about Sloane being spotted at the Eiffel Tower. If he was going to visit New York, just hypothetically, he would definitely be caught on camera somehow. She felt a little better knowing that.

When the elevator landed with its indicator tone, the two women and the timid pooch, now shaking, stepped inside. Becka pressed eleven and double-tapped her phone.

"Crap!" she expelled, startling the dog and her owner. "Oh, sorry!"

The text was from the police.

A few rumbly seconds later, she got off the elevator and let herself into her apartment. What a mess of a day. She'd never been grilled by the police before and it was unsettling. A nice bubble bath and takeout would certainly help.

After tossing her messenger bag onto the dining room "table"—a tiny café-style two-top made of the finest double plywood—she hit the bathroom, peeling off her work clothes and starting the bath. While she waited for it to fill up, she put on some booty shorts (nobody was going to see her anyway) and a black ribbed tank top, then sank into her recliner with an audible groan. The chair was the only furniture she had ever spent any kind of money on. Plush and dreamy, it was totally worth the $1K she'd shelled out. Her mother droned on about it being an unnecessary indulgence and a waste of money. What could you expect from a Depression-era baby? Self-care hadn't been invented yet.

With an eye on the time—in about two minutes, the bath would be ready—her finger hovered over the text bubble.

The sender was "SHEEPBAY PRECINCT."

Please call Officers Kline/Frost, thank you.

"What? Already?" she said out loud. "Okay, buddy. Let's get this over with." She touched the phone icon.

"Officer Justin Kline, K-L-I-N-E, here."

Why did he have to do this every time?

"Hi, Officer. This is Becka Rifkin."

"Thank you for calling me back. We just have a few more questions for you. Can you come to the stationhouse on Avenue Z? I work the day shift from Tuesday to Sunday, seven to three-thirty."

"Well, I guess I'm in luck. Tomorrow morning looks doable." There was no smile in her voice.

"Sounds good."

"Quick question."

"Yes?"

"Frankly, am I going to be arrested or something?" *You know, like, should I get a lawyer?*

"No, I guarantee you, no arrests happening." The delivery was deadpan.

She clicked off without saying goodbye. It was enough today of everybody.

Becka took off her shorts and tank top and flicked off the faucet. White mounds of foam gave off the scent of gardenias. If she wasn't getting arrested, whatever was going to happen shouldn't take too long. That would be tomorrow's headache, anyway, along with yet a second day of training.

The end was near, she thought, for Pyotr, Sloane, Kline, Lizzy, the bunch of them.

Becka thought long and hard about bringing something special to her seven a.m. "appointment" at the police station—Ms. Dinah Shore.

The worst that could happen would be that they'd confiscate the record. Which might be the best outcome after all. It would take the troublesome item off her hands and out of her life. If Sloane ever came sniffing around (though he was probably being shipped to an isolated shack in the tundra), she could honestly say she didn't have it anymore. They couldn't arrest her for stealing it; it had been paid for (with an added and inconvenient little detail of perhaps Becka partaking in some money laundering). And it wasn't contraband, because, well, the Cold War was over, last she looked.

As for the other, more troublesome, bone record? Poor little Uliana Stalin. It was a gruesome, sad story. If she'd only gotten the medical help she needed and been loved and cherished like a child should be, who knows? She could have had a beautiful life as a dancer or a photojournalist.

At least the X-ray Becka owned was anonymous. The less she knew about the cursed thing, the better, and she'd soon be getting rid of it one way or the other.

Whoever stole Jerry Zolotov's bone record had to be on the run. They probably were long gone in some unpronounceable jurisdiction and the record would wait until the investigation cooled off. It could have already been sold on the dark web.

“Miss Rifkin.” Officer Justin Kline stepped up to the counter. “I’ll buzz you in.”

Becka squinted out the harsh lights above. And then the smells hit her full-on. A mélange of sweat, anxiety and disappointment, plus the ghost of half-eaten lunches of every international cuisine. Pizza boxes were piled on desks and fried chicken buckets perched on top of overflowing trash bins. Clouds of used napkins littered nearly every surface.

“Thanks for coming. This way,” he said.

Eyes the color of the ocean on a calm day.

Becka followed the officer up a flight of stairs and along a bright corridor into a small room. A window embedded with chicken wire looked out onto Ocean Avenue. Lines of eastbound traffic snaked to the beaches and ultimately to Long Island. In the other direction, lane closures clogged up the flow of traffic, with an ambulance trying to thread its way into Manhattan.

Suddenly, Becka got an idea. Just in case he said yes, she had to ask, but it was a long shot.

“Can I record this with my phone?”

He pulled back and laughed. It sounded like a bark. “You don’t watch many cop shows, do you?” A slight pinkness came over his neck.

“I guess that was a stupid thing to ask.”

He flashed her a smile. His top teeth were like Chicklets, pure white, nice and square. Implants, she guessed. The bottom teeth were crowded in together, the middle two pushed slightly forward. Those were his real ones.

"Not at all, Miss—"

"Rifkin, but call me Becka."

She sat on a cheap metal chair and put a cardboard tube on the desk. The room, though bare, felt grimier and more unsettling than the rest of the precinct.

"We have private 'chats' here, in case you're wondering. If you were a real suspect, Officer Frost would be here with me. You want me to call her in?"

He was asking her about procedures? The door was open, putting her at ease, so Becka shook her head.

"You're not a suspect, of course. We just think you might have some information that we'll find useful. But I know your type, so...."

"What type is that?"

"Why, the innocent type." He sure hoped he was right on that one, or Frost would have his ass.

She looked down and suppressed a smile, realizing that the flirtation was going two ways.

Officer Kline hiked his chin to the cardboard tube. "So, what's that?"

"It's my bone record."

"Of course. Can I get a look at it?"

Becka pried off the cap with her fingernail and lightly slid out the film curled up inside.

"Be careful, it's really brittle. When I first put it into the tube, an edge cracked off. I nearly freaked out."

"Don't worry, it's your baby. I get it."

"Seriously, this wasn't a cheap proposition. That little tiny corner cost me about fifty dollars."

All that money down the drain.

"How much did you pay for it?"

Was this regular curiosity or part of her "unofficial" questioning?

"Seven hundred fifty."

When the record was fully removed, she placed it on the desk blotter in front of her.

"May I?" he asked.

She nodded.

Kline put on latex gloves and gently pinched the left and right sides of the X-ray before holding it up to the window.

"Holy shiiiit! Look at this. A jawbone! Teeth knocked out! This is wild!"

Becka felt morbidly proud.

"Can I take a picture?" he asked.

"Go ahead."

"I don't have a light table or anything, so can you hold it in front of the window? If you don't mind."

She got up and carefully took it from him, sensing the warmth of his fingers through the gloves. She walked over to the window and held up the film.

"Do you want to buy a vowel?" she asked.

That bark again. "Ah, a kindred spirit. My favorite show with takeout. Maybe sometime we can watch it together."

Surely Officer Frost would not have approved of that comment.

Kline snapped a photo of it and smiled. "I have a picture of a real bone record—I actually touched a real bone record! What would Eva think!"

"Who's Eva?"

"My mom. She was a real jazz lover. She would have loved to see Dinah Shore on stage. My mom comped in a few ensembles in the fifties. A master on the keys and a vocalist, too."

"Oh, so that's how you knew about Buddy Rich and—"

"Bunny Berigan. Yup."

Becka sat back down. This was a waste of time. He obviously just wanted to see the record.

"You can pack it up again. Thanks for bringing it."

"I thought you guys were going to confiscate it."

"Eva might have loved Miss Shore, but the NYPD? Couldn't give a hot damn. Even with a killer on the loose."

That quickly sobered things up.

"Do you have a suspect?" she asked super casually.

"In the killing or the burglary?"

Becka hadn't heard about a burglary. Maybe Pyotr didn't know either.

"Oh, I didn't hear about that."

Kline smiled and figured it wouldn't hurt to tell her. "Seems like somebody was casing the place first and then did the deed. Must have been in-between shifts over at Zolotov's place right after he died. Which is strange, since the Mossad guy was pretty much living there, even though he was told he couldn't be there during the investigation."

"So no suspects for that or the murder?"

"We haven't established if it *is* murder. But I hear what you're asking. We have a few people we're talking to. But I can't say anything else about it. You wanna get me fired?" He smiled.

"No, Officer, I wouldn't want to do that."

He asked her some more about her trip to Russia and if there was anything else about Jerry Zolotov she wanted to say. She repeated what she had told them before, that the closest she ever came to meeting him was thinking about buying tickets to see him with her mother. The thought stilled her and she shook it off.

"His house is right here in Manhattan Beach. I never knew that until I heard what happened to him."

"Well, you couldn't have gotten too close anyway, even if you were a determined fan. He had these really tall shrubs around the house and lining the driveway. From the other homes in the neighborhood, you wouldn't be able to guess that a driveway could be that long. And a private security force from Mossad or something."

To Becka's surprise, he took out a box of cigarettes from his pants pocket. He pulled out a slim filtered one and put it in his mouth, unlit.

"Trying to kick it. I'm having trouble giving up the ritual."

Becka looked past him to the doorway. She needed to get to work and hadn't counted on taking a detour. She'd have to drop off the bone record at home first.

"Tell me about Sloane. And don't worry, this won't take much longer. I appreciate you coming in, and I know you need to get to the hospital. What time, by the way?"

“I start at nine, but I need to bring this home quick.”

“So, Sloane?”

Becka launched into a physical description, complete with his disgusting beard, wiry sideburns and permanent scowl. She told him how he behaved in a threatening manner toward Pyotr. Her heart did double-time at the mention of his name.

“I’m actually right now deciding who to return this to. I know if I keep it, I’ll never get any peace. That creep might come looking for it.”

Kline studied the flecks of light brown in her eyes and briefly looked at her mouth. “What about that Sofia lady you told us about? What’s her last name? And this Silvan Sloane character—I’d bet the house that’s not his real name.”

“So long as the record doesn’t boomerang back to me, I don’t care what her real name is. And him? Honestly, the less I know, the better.”

Satisfied that he got all he needed, he tapped the table twice and got up.

“Ms. Rifkin, thank you for stopping in.”

Becka nodded with finality. “See you.”

As she turned to leave, he whistled a tune. It was the opening strain of Gershwin’s “Isn’t it Romantic.” She walked out without letting him see her smile.

Gloria Frost was suddenly in the doorway. “Are we getting familiar with our suspects?” she asked.

“Nah. She’s no suspect. Which is unfortunate, because now I don’t have a reason to call her in again.”

The next morning, Gloria Frost clicked her locker closed and smoothed down her uniform. Nine more years of this stuff.

It wasn't as if she hated her job. Quite the opposite. She just hoped to get out of it alive. All well and good to interview people she pretty much knew were innocent; investigating somebody like Becka Rifkin was cake. But add some Eastern European mafia types into the mix and, frankly, she was terrified. Brooklyn had its bad neighborhoods but Brighton Beach wasn't one of them. However, Little Odessa was quietly starting to climb the list. Dotted with "unsolved" murders that this year numbered twelve, she had every reason to be on her guard.

"Hey Kline, with a K-L-I-N and an E. Wassup?"

As usual, the guy was eating. Crumbs from a donut fell from his face.

"Hey, pardner." He lifted his half-eaten donut in greeting. "We're closer to an answer on the Jerry Z case."

"That fast?" Frost had brought in an egg and cheese on a toasted sesame bagel from the corner deli. Much more sensible than a fistful of sugar.

"Didn't you hear?" he asked her.

"No. I was caught up in getting my son from the airport. He just came home from college. And he's moving back in." She looked heavenward and smiled.

"Mazel tov...right?"

"Yeah, I love having my baby back," she said. "Earl and I are happier than pigs in slop. Now, of course, the kid has to look for a job. But tell me about the case. I can't believe you didn't text me, Kline!"

"Hey, cool your jets. It just came in overnight. Tox got a shot at the body."

"And?"

"Something called pentium phosphorus. In its liquid form, it's lethal. Like immediately."

"I don't get it. What was the primary cause of death?"

Kline opened a white paper bag. The donut was only his warm-up.

"Ramirez, dammit! Didn't I tell you NO pickles? I got the hypah-tension!" He peeled off the offending garnish.

From the next room, he heard: "Hey Kline, you knew I was going to the Cuban place on Brighton 2. Next time, tell me. And no, you didn't actually mention the pickles."

Frost sat on Kline's desk and glared at him. "Do I have to be in your face? Tell me what happened!"

"Oh, sorry," he said, dropping the pickles into the garbage. "So this pentium, it causes immediate disorientation and then you're at death's door. There's no time to act unless somebody happens to be there at the exact moment of consumption, and then you have to try to get them to vomit."

"Hmm. And it was slick there on the walkway."

"Exactly. They didn't think he was pushed. He was really good friends with this other musician, Stewie

Goldmann, that the Midtown cops are on. But he wouldn't have made sense for this. No motive."

Frost nodded. "So what did Tox say about the source?"

"The stuff comes from Eastern Europe. I suppose anybody can get anything from the internet, but interesting that our Sloane guy was a hot figure in this case and of course he's based in St. Petersburg. Basically, they're saying the poor sucker was poisoned and then actually legit slipped."

"His friend couldn't grab him in time?" Frost asked.

"Stewie Goldmann? Frail as a pretzel. They were childhood friends. Sad."

"That doesn't necessarily rule him out," Frost observed.

"Well...Zolotov gave him a kidney in '99. They're essentially brothers. But I guess it could happen."

"We going to tie things up with that girl Becka?"

"Yeah, I'd love to—never mind."

Frost threw her balled-up wrapper at him. "Behave!"

"I'll try. She was cute."

"I will ignore that comment, Officer. You going to update her so she knows she's officially off the hook?"

"Yeah, don't worry. I work fast."

Frost closed her long-lashed eyes and shook her head. "Lord, I know you do."

Becka made it to the conference room on time for the next training session, still on the new machines. She was wiped out. The training, dealing with the police, rehashing her encounters with Sloane and trying to forget Pyotr; all that combined, and her stress levels were off the chart.

As the sun streamed in through the floor-to-ceiling windows of the fifth-floor conference room, she grabbed a cherry Danish and a cup of tea and slinked to her seat. She saw a slice of that beautiful Atlantic Ocean. Somebody passed her the sign-in sheet and the handouts, and somewhere between her first sip of tea and salivating for her Danish, her phone went off. Loudly.

"Sorry!"

She got an eyeful from the presenter. "Thank you for leaving your phone off, puh-lease."

Oh relax, Miss Prissy, she thought. *It's obvious the hospital is about to shell out beaucoup bucks for your big, fancy machines. Just do your damn presentation.*

But her phone wouldn't stop buzzing. She was about to muffle it in her laptop bag and put the bag on the floor when she realized it was Pyotr blowing up her phone.

"Excuse me." Biting off a chunk of the pastry because she was starving, she quickly stepped out of the room, getting a rueful look as she went.

Her boss would have her neck for this. But truth be told, she'd get up to speed on this stuff easy-peasy.

Anything she missed would either be in the materials they handed out or on the hospital's intranet.

We have to talk

Hi sweetie! How about hello my waffle or something?

No time for the kidding

What's up? You're starting to scare me.

Interpol is involved and they brought me in

Her body turned to granite. *OMG did they hurt you? They asked about Sloane?*

Yes. I mean no hurting, that's just in the movies, but yes

OK but you didn't even know Jerry Zolotov! Why are you freaking out?

Her eyes were fused to the screen. It stayed blank for about thirty seconds, which normally wasn't long for a casual conversation, but considering the circumstances, it was terrifying. She salivated, the first sign that throwing up was a real possibility.

P! Why r u freaking--

They said not to leave the country, they might need me around

Becka had a feeling deep in her gut. Her glial cells were telling her "abort mission."

Pyotr had never divulged exactly what he did for a living. It was clear as mud that the subject was off-limits. She immediately understood she had no rights to the information. She wouldn't pry then and she wasn't going to ask for transparency now. No sense in it.

As a hookup, Pyotr was a match made in heaven. The problem was that it wasn't just a hot little diversion. Becka had started to catch feelings.

P, if this doesn't have to do exactly with -

She hesitated before completing her text.

me and Dinah, maybe I -

Maybe you should ask me not to continue talking to you about it. Ya?

Thank God Pyotr got it. The need-to-know basis? She wasn't in that inner circle. And maybe now was the precise time to start thinking of her experiences with the handsome "broker," or whatever he called himself, as something in the past.

What are you going to do? She couldn't help it.

I told you let's not talk about it

Are you in danger?

My sweet little American blintz with honey on top, I adore you

Now Becka was thoroughly confused.

Are you messing with me?

No, the police and Interpol are really on this case. They are on Sloane's tail too. But he can't be found. So the less you know, the better.

He was AWOL? Becka had two choices. She could swipe to her main screen to leave the conversation and block his number with a quiet, unobtrusive finger tap, and then change her number and make all her socials private. That wasn't going to happen. Or she could keep him at arm's length, not block him, but trust that he wouldn't involve her anymore. Just let him fade away into the ether. That made more sense. Unfortunately, her heart was sending signals to her brain that melted all logic.

My advice is to not contact SS. Block him. And you paid for the book, yes?

You're like my mom! Yes!

What a tangled web. Purchasing the record through the phony book transaction was money laundering. There was no getting away from that. Interpol would most definitely love to get their hands on international money fuckery.

Becka, I need to go resolve things with Sloane right now, if I can find him.

It was as good a time as any to make an exit. Click "off" and walk back to the conference room. But she didn't.

He continued.

Maybe some days or weeks have to pass before we talk again, OK? BTW are you sexy right now?

She almost screamed in confusion, but she remembered she was still at work.

Pyotr! The LAST thing I feel is sexy!

OK ha, see I got you to laugh. We'll talk again. Till then xoxo

As she was about to silence her phone once more and shift it to her back pocket, it buzzed again. A call this time.

Officer Justin Kline.

There was only one thing to do.

Ignore it.

“Sloane is suspect number one for that break-in.” Officer Kline was looking at a few takeout menus, but he’d already decided on Italian. He cracked open a can of Diet Pepsi and got ready to tell Ramirez what to pick up for him.

Gloria Frost was setting down her napkins for a warm knish with extra yellow mustard. “More than likely it was him. And since he just ran out on bail, I’m sure he left France. He could be here in New York. The FBI won’t share anything with us so who knows?”

“I just hope he’s not on that girl Becka Rifkin’s tail for her bone record.”

Frost caught a softness in his voice. “Jeez. You could tell she was terrified he might come for her.”

“How does this even happen?” Kline said. “I mean, like a schmuck, Jerry Z goes and takes a little 2 a.m. drive to the Verrazano in the rain.” He shook his head. “Gets out, and then goes over to the walkway and poof! I mean, stupid or suicidal?”

“Maybe we’ll never know.”

“And Sloane walked right into the lion’s den. Coming to New York, breaking in—let’s say—then God knows where Zolotov’s Mossad musclehead was. Then assaulting this little old mystery writer in Paris, with all that goddamn surveillance? A big mistake.”

“The mistake was the French cops let him go.” Frost was still incredulous.

The delivery guy left a brown paper bag at the counter and Kline nodded, handing him a twenty and a five and shaking his head for no change back.

"Man, I'm starving." He unwrapped his monster meatball hero. Hypertension was nipping at his heels, or so his doctor said. He didn't pry it open to add salt, but he wanted to.

"You gonna eat that whole thing?" Frost asked him.

"Thanks for asking. Yes, I am. And what'd you get?"

"A knish." She pronounced it "*nish*."

"Gloria! How long've you been on this green earth? It's *kuh-nish*. I'm taking away your New York credentials."

"Okay, okay." She smiled. Thank God she had pulled him as a partner. She could've gotten one of the racist idiots the precinct was notorious for. Small miracles do happen.

Just then, a call came through on the old landline on Officer Kline's desk.

"You don't say. Wow. Okay." He looked up. "Speak of the damned devil. So Becka might have had cause to worry, but not anymore. Sloane—real name Silwan Poretsky—was just picked up in London and his ass has been deported back to Moscow. With what's happening now in that part of the world, he's not coming back anytime soon. Or maybe ever."

Maybe I should tell Becka that her archnemesis was just shipped back home in handcuffs. She's free to go about her life. Yeah, I should probably let her know.

The new machines at Shore Unity Hospital were soon being used all around the tri-state region. Becka found herself logging mileage onto her trip sheets for every little corner of Brooklyn and New Jersey. On Friday, she had one more visit scheduled to the hospital in southeastern Connecticut.

The pre-Christmas chill (balmy in comparison to St. Petersburg) had set in and she'd gotten herself a new down overcoat, which she wished she had a few weeks ago. So long ago, it felt like a million years.

She walked to her rental car in the humongous parking lot at Quinnipiac Hospital, right along the river of the same name. A rental was the only way to make these trips, and with the car covered plus mileage, parking and a small lunch budget, it wasn't a bad way to get out of the office for the day.

By 4 p.m., her job was done and she wanted to book before it got dark, but the radiology department head was a pontificator. Twenty minutes later, Becka found herself breaking the conversation mid-sentence to get on the road. She wouldn't get back in time to return the car for the day, but the hospital would pick up the next day's slightly higher Saturday rates. So be it.

A two-hour hour commute home lay in front of her, and she'd need to tack on another twenty minutes to find a spot in her neighborhood. Already she needed a new vacation. This time, one without the international intrigue.

With the Q River to her right and a cold half-cup of Earl Grey tea still in her console from the morning, she put on a smooth jazz radio station. There was a tribute to the late Jerry Zolotov. His music was just the thing she needed to unwind on the drive home. There was a song called "So Right and Right On" that had a funky element. Whoever was on the bass was a master.

From the little she picked up in the media, Zolotov resented any musicians, even his own band members, who were better than him, but because his band's image was also so important, he only chose the best musicians. So he was kind of a walking conundrum.

The time was a smidge before six o'clock. She could almost feel the relief of tearing off her bra. As she exited the highway and onto the streets of Sheepshead Bay, she saw a spot in front of a Chinese restaurant that she had passed on the way in.

"Beef and carrots. No broccoli. Brown rice, not white. Thanks."

The young woman behind the acrylic partition smiled.

"And an egg roll, please."

In twelve minutes, Becka was trawling the last few blocks before getting to her building. Aromas filled the car and there was nobody saying she couldn't drive and eat an egg roll at the same time.

The parking gods heard her prayers and she pulled into the smallest possible spot on Bay 24th Street. With her fragrant dinner in a plastic bag in one hand and her phone and pepper spray in the other, she half-ran for three blocks and landed in her apartment lobby.

There were Christmas lights on a tired plastic tree and the mailbox wall was full of peach-colored notes from the post office about missed deliveries.

Almost bra-shedding time.

Her phone buzzed as she stepped into the elevator. It was Pyotr.

This better be a fun and flirty call, she thought. Becka had no bandwidth for anything else, least of all an update on a murder case.

Zoom me, the text read.

5 minutes? she replied.

She fumbled with her dinner, her messenger bag getting in the way of her keys.

When she got up to eleven and into her apartment, she peeled off her coat and hung it on the closet doorknob, stripped down to her undies, and went to the bathroom. Then she scrubbed her face with a soapy washcloth and dried it with a fresh, fluffy towel.

Her dining room table was a speck, not big enough for the laptop and dinner; it was one or the other. She pulled over a rickety snack table, something she'd salvaged from her mother's apartment, opened her laptop and logged in.

"Hello, my sweetheart! I love seeing that face," Pyotr said warmly.

He looked amazing. Handsome, windblown, eyes sparkling.

"Well, hello yourself. I hope you don't mind me eating. I just drove back from Connecticut. Two hours! So to what do I owe the pleasure of seeing you tonight?

I take it based on your smile that everything with Interpol has been resolved?"

A forkful of beef with brown rice and a carrot sliver made her hum in appreciation. Her whole body relaxed.

"I'm afraid I have bad news."

"What? What's the matter?" She stopped chewing.

Pyotr shook his head. "I just need to tell you, uh, that we won't be talking for, uh, quite the while."

"You told me that last time. What happened now?" Suddenly, the appetite that got her to Brooklyn in under two hours was gone just like that.

"Sofia and I have to go away for a time. We will be, eh, relocating."

"Why? Hold on. You and Sofia? Are you, like, together?" Disgust made its way up Becka's throat. "What the actual...."

"NO! Becka, no. She is—she is my sister."

Becka lost a few grains of rice from her mouth as her jaw opened. She wanted to talk but didn't know what to say.

"I know this is a shock. But hear me out. Something happened, and we have to leave."

"Okay, Pyotr, either you come clean right now or I will freakin' end this call and never talk to you again. I mean EVER."

In quiet tones, Pyotr began explaining that he hadn't been totally honest with her. Sofia was his sister and they were working together. It had started with a 16rpm record of Thad Jones on the Blue Note label that an American friend of Sofia's had left behind in their apartment back in 1998. Before they knew it, it had progressed to the bone records and lost, stolen or mysteriously acquired Western rarities like uncirculated baseball cards, hood ornaments, jewelry, instruments, anything they could fence.

"You fooled me into buying the bone record so...so what? So you and Sofia could steal it back?"

"No. It wasn't supposed to happen that way. I knew how special this was to you. You were not to be touched. Then Silwan Poretsky butted his fat head into it and—"

"You mean Silvan? Sloane?"

"Well, you must've known that wasn't his real name. It's *Silwan*. Yes."

"Wait, he's one of you? You're working together?"

"That was why I knew he wouldn't actually hurt you or force you to give it up. You were off-limits."

"You mean the three of you are going to relocate?" she asked, mouth dry.

"No. Just me and Sofia."

So Silvan was still on the lam. It didn't matter what Pyotr said next. Becka was terrified all over again.

"This is crazy!" she said. "You are SUCH an asshole! I'm ending this call. Don't you ever contact me again! And you tell your partner Silvan or Silwan or whatever his name is to leave me the fuck alone!"

"Silwan's dead."

Becka couldn't believe her ears. "What!! What happened?"

Pyotr looked away. His eyes were wet. He swiped a sleeve over his face and told Becka the truth.

Sofia and Silvan were married, but only for convenience. With the valuable merchandise they were dealing with, being married made things easier with the government. If one of them were to die, the surviving spouse would inherit all the "marital proceeds," but if they were not married, ownership of the property would have to be ascertained by a special police unit. In the meantime, everything would become the property of the state—and this often took years to sift through and resolve, if ever.

"Okay, so they were, uh, married."

That didn't quite square with Becka. This was getting crazier every second.

"Yeah," he continued to Becka's silence. "My sister went with him to a nightclub last night. And—" Pyotr's voice broke. He hung his head and sobbed.

"Oh my God, what happened?"

"Silwan is—was—a very jealous man. Even though the marriage was just on paper, he was...I think he was actually in love with my sister."

"And?"

"He caught her looking—smiling, really—at somebody else. A woman. He became enraged. It wasn't the first time."

My intuition about her being gay was right on point, Becka thought. *What a narcissist for Silvan to think he could "woo her away" from being attracted to women!*

"When they got home, Silwan went crazy and.... Uh, I cannot say this."

"Pyotr! I hope she's okay?"

"He brutalized her. At least, he tried to. She ran to the night table and took out a pistol." He cleared his throat and blew his nose. "He was a scumbag anyway. We all knew that. Even you."

"When you say scumbag, do you mean...look, did he kill Jerry Zolotov?"

"Impossible. Sofia agrees with me on this. He came to Brooklyn to steal the Stalin record, yes. He broke in. He is very good—he was very good—with hacking home security systems, even with that Israeli around. But he worked alone on those jobs and couldn't have known that Jerry was going to the Verrazano Bridge. Silwan would have broken in with Zolotov at home or not, it didn't matter. He was stealthy like a cat. I hear that he returned to St. Pete with the X-ray of Stalin's baby, may the little girl's soul rest in peace."

"Hold on. Who pushed him over the railing, then?

"My darling, I have no idea."

"Silvan's body, though...?"

"You should not ask such things. But we have to go now. I am so sorry to lay this at your feet. I really care about you."

This is how it ends? She had a much more benign conclusion in mind.

"Some other time, we could have been nice for one another. I should tell you that I'm using a burner phone so you won't be able to get me again. I'm so sorry."

Tears streamed down Becka's face. She couldn't think of anything to say. She loved a liar, a thief and an admitted accomplice to murder, but Silvan's murder, not Jerry's.

"Please consider this my sweet kiss goodbye to you." He pressed his fingers tenderly to his lips and touched his camera lens.

"I don't know what to say."

"Say 'be safe, take care of Sofia, and I love you.' Because that's what I'll say to you. My sweetheart. I love you, Becka."

Unable to meet his eyes, Becka whispered, "I love you, too."

The officer who loved to spell his name couldn't get that Rifkin woman out of his head. He confided in his partner about it.

"You know Sergeant Bloom says she's not on the list," Officer Gloria Frost said one morning, picking up the trash on the desks and giving dirty looks to the other officers. She crumpled up a sandwich wrapper and lobbed it at Ramirez, who finally got the idea to pitch in. "Go ask her out. You have my blessings."

"She's cute, right?" Kline smiled and looked at his phone. Her number, which he should have deleted, was under "Brown-Eyed Girl."

He thought about bodies falling over railings. *We never know when it's our time.* There was a spark there, and he wanted to explore it.

Two days later, Becka agreed to meet at the diner again. This time, not for questioning.

She tapped her wrist. "I've got one hour and I have a wicked appetite for some French toast. So bring me up to date. Please." She smiled.

Kline was ecstatic about having breakfast with her. She was adorable and all dressed up for work. All business. There was definitely a soft side somewhere in there too.

"I was at the search right after the break-in. No bone record, of course. That sucker is long gone." Justin sipped his coffee, not enjoying how the scorching hot felt on his top lip.

Becka nodded. “I can only wonder where that record is now.”

“I have an idea.”

“Oh?”

“It’s you. You’re the mastermind. We found your prints all over it, so...I’m gonna pull out my handcuffs.” He laughed.

“Yeah, try again, Officer. And ixnay on the cuffs. At least for now.”

He put his hand on hers. It was warm. She blushed and turned it over, lacing her fingers in his.

“The record most likely found its way back to your, um, boyfriend.” He waited for some reaction or clarification.

Nothing. But she didn’t pull her hand away.

“Whoever it is, the thing is nowhere to be found,” he continued. “All that money Jerry put into it, and not just the record but the artwork, the frame. I saw pictures. Crazy stuff. A colossal waste of money, if you ask me. You got one for what, like seven hundred fifty bucks?”

“Yep, and a lot of heartache. Like it was cursed. The whole bone records industry. Madness.” She looked at the crinkles around his eyes as he smiled.

“Did you know that his body, when they did the autopsy—”

Becka held up a hand. “Let’s just skip the gruesome parts.”

He pulled back. “Fair enough.”

“Go on.”

“The evidence was that he’d been poisoned.”

"Yeah, I read something about that. But who pushed him?"

"That's the thing. His childhood friend Stew Goldmann wasn't charged or even suspected. The real question is, who poisoned him in the first place? Sloane might have broken in and stolen the record, but the sax Jerry died with wasn't at his home at the time of the break-in, at least according to his bodyguard."

"He had enemies, or so I've heard," she mused. "Doesn't every celebrity? Even smooth jazz artists?"

"Especially smooth jazz artists. Ask any bebopper."

The next week, Officer Kline was up for another breakfast date. He also had something to tell Becka.

He texted about meeting at their favorite diner as soon as she was available.

At seven or a bit before if you can. I'm doing 8s this week for some unknown reason.

Seven a.m. was pretty damn early, but Becka was up then anyway and didn't need to be in for another two hours. It would be great to tie up loose ends, especially if he was going to tell her they got the killer. She was curious about the details of the case. About him, too.

She got there first and took a booth along the back wall, already knowing she'd move to the other side of it so he'd have a view of the entrance.

"Good morning, sunshine!"

"Good morning back. Did you eat already?" She smiled warmly.

"That's a joke, right? You think all I do is stuff my face with donuts back at the precinct with all those motley characters?"

"I love the Bavarian cream ones the most."

Officer Kline wrestled out of his nylon jacket. It looked like a full-body toolbelt. Walkie-talkie that crackled incessantly, a long black flashlight, gleaming chrome handcuffs and other devices not easy to identify. His jacket clunked when he dropped it onto the bench seat. He tugged at his collar and Becka could see a stiff Kevlar vest underneath his blues.

"Wait, are we back to me being interrogated?" she asked with a smirk.

"Do you want to be?"

Ah. Teasing me again.

"Do you always answer..."

"Yes I do. And no, it's not. An interrogation. Those days are over. So, we having breakfast?"

"Just a bagel with a shmear and a tea for me," Becka said.

"Okay, I'll just have the biggest omelet they got. All the meats."

After they ordered, he tilted the cow-shaped creamer over his coffee and made a few swirling motions.

"I have an interesting update for you." He sipped and the coffee scalded his lip. Every time. Did he not learn? "That guy Pyotr isn't a suspect, but let's just say he's in big international trouble."

Becka was stunned, but she played it cool. She didn't expect her now-former boyfriend to enter the conversation.

"You were pretty much hanging around with a big player in the underground bootleg shit going on there. Not sure you knew the extent of it, but I'm just sayin'." Kline bore his gaze into Becka and waited.

"You mean, I was sleeping with...."

"Yup, the enemy. But I ain't your mama, Rifkin."

If she wasn't so totally confused about Pyotr and who he really was, she would have found Kline's calling her by her last name very sexy. But she had a lot to sort out, so she let the moment pass.

"All I'm saying is that it's a good thing you're here and he's there."

"Do you think I'm in danger?" she asked. *Here we go again*!

"I seriously doubt it. Besides, he really liked you, right?" Kline's ears turned pink. "I don't suppose he gave you the inside scoop on his 'work' activities?"

Pyotr had said nothing, so Becka knew nothing. Thanks be to God.

"He said I wouldn't want to know. I guess he was right. Any leads on the poisoning?"

"We have some ideas. I can't talk about them. But what about your X-ray record?" He chuckled. "It was pretty awesome that you scored one. Honestly, I'd love to hear it, uh, sometime."

Maybe he was angling for some sort of invitation, but again, different channel altogether. With this new information, Becka's mind was trying to close the chapter with Pyotr. She didn't know what *this* right here might be, with Kline, or Justin, as she should really call him if they were going to see each other, but she hoped it was the start of something.

"I ended up shipping it back to him, in fact. Now, wherever the winds or seas take it, it's out of my life and I couldn't be happier."

"Ah, a shame. But I understand. Did you get to listen to it, at least?"

"I didn't have the chance. I was going to look up how to play it without ruining it. As soon as I realized what a huge cluster this whole ordeal was, I couldn't wait to get it off my hands. But if you ask me if I regret not playing it, yeah, I do."

They finished their breakfasts in silence. Becka turned around to look at the gigantic cookies in the glass displays up front. On the way out, she could get one chocolate chip to go and slice it into quarters for her next few lunches at work.

She took out her wallet and smiled charmingly. Considering what she'd just learned, it would be best to keep her Soviet lover as an ex. And Kline, or *Justin*, well, that had yet to be explored.

The MRI machines over in Shore Unity's Jersey contingent were having problems. It would take all week to sort them out. Millstone General was twenty minutes from Jeff's house.

I wonder how he is.

No, I don't.

She got to the parking lot a half-hour early. A good spot near the front. It was raw and gray and the air smelled like a January snow.

As a small-town offshoot hospital, Millstone had a modest radiology department. Two ultrasound machines, each about ten years old, had to be checked. Becka would run through a series of tests and communicate back to her boss, then wait for them to be used in mock sessions by the staff throughout the week. Only after they were proven to be operable could she then sign off.

She kept her car running for heat. With time to spare and just because it popped into her head, she dialed Suzanne, who answered right away.

"Hey, girlfriend! What's going on?"

Becka summarized her trip to Russia. She didn't leave out her former heartthrob.

"Sounds amazing. And I heard about that international intrigue, huh! I hope it didn't get in the way of your trip."

"Was that really all over the news here? It was pretty freaky, I'll say that." Suddenly, Becka didn't feel friendless.

"Yup, it's been a big deal. Anyway, so weird you should call me. Jeff's been talking about reaching out to you."

"I just silently groaned, in case you didn't hear it."

"Yeah, well, he was worried about you," Suzanne said. "I think he wants to see if you're interested in getting back together."

"What?"

"Well, if you do, and it's none of my beeswax, he's more than willing to take you back."

"Take ME back? What a historical revisionist. If that's a thing."

"It is. I take it you're not interested?" Suzanne asked.

"Right you are. You know how he is."

"Boy, do I."

It was time to get going. "I'll just tell you that things were okay until they weren't...until he had all these women from work calling him, and not just during the day. Besides, there's your little guy Cody. It's such a responsibility on the girlfriend when there's a kid in the picture. It would be too painful for him if things didn't work out with Jeff again, and it's just not right to put him through that."

"Wow," Suzanne said. Becka could hear her go quiet. "That's very thoughtful, thank you. Cody's a sensitive kid. The whole dating thing leaves a strong impression and these years are too tender to play around with."

"Exactly. Hey, I gotta run and find the lockers and everything. It's a new hospital for me."

"Where are you?"

"Millstone."

"No way! If you're still there on Friday, I can pop over and meet you at the cafeteria for lunch."

"It's a date."

The parking lot had a sign for open houses in the nearby development of Farris Hills. That was where Lizzy lived. Becka was going to have to nullify that piece of data and move on with her life.

Sandra's therapy sessions had Rozina DuPont in a better frame of mind. She felt more equipped to handle her bad days by compartmentalizing all the issues going on at once. For about a month after Jerry's death, Eric kept asking her how she was feeling. He thought he was giving her space, but he always had to be in her head.

"Enough! Please, Eric. I can't keep checking my emotional barometer every time you think I'm looking sad."

A serious look came over his face and he shook his head. "I'm going to the sunroom with my coffee. Join me if you want. Might be our last winter here, if you're still interested in moving to the Panhandle."

She felt bad for snapping at him. He was looking out for her. Reminding her about Florida made her heart skip a beat, in a good way. Getting out of the Northeast for good was something they talked about doing when she retired. But it was too much at the moment. One thing at a time.

"I'll come with you."

Over the last three weeks, Sandra had helped Rozina find the words to explain to Eric how to back off, but by doing it kindly. Finally, he understood that what she needed wasn't for him to stop noticing her moods, but to stop reporting on them.

"Hey, look in the mail tray," he said mysteriously, making a kissy face.

"Mmm, after this cup." She sipped noisily. "This chai you got last week is really spicy, but it's hitting me right. So what are you doing today, hun?"

"Well, it's tied into that surprise. When you see it, I'll tell you what I'm doing today. I think you'll approve."

She walked into the foyer and went to the mail tray. There was a glossy orange envelope with a stylized logo of a ship. She immediately thought about Sandy, who'd recently told her, "You need to have some good old, balls-out fun in life. Honor your grief when you need to. There will always be private times to do that. Trust me, it'll get easier."

A cruise, but to where? She put down her cup and slid her finger under the flap of the envelope. Out came two jumbo candy bar-sized packets, stapled together.

Join us for some smooth jazz on the beautiful open seas!

Rozina's first reaction was disappointment chased by annoyance and then anger. Why would he want to bring her to an event that would remind her of Jerry? Then she became depressed. Everyone was going to be talking about what happened to Jerry Zolotov, each one of them with their own opinion about his death. What a terrible idea this was.

She set her face right and took a deep inhale. Watching in the mirror for a smile to appear, she got ready to thank Eric for the tickets. How much fun a jazz cruise was going to be! After all, she did really love the music.

Just then, her phone went off. She patted the back pocket of her jeans, but her phone was quiet. Then she looked at the breakfront across the foyer and saw his phone light up.

I'll bring him his phone.

In over forty years of marriage, she'd never looked through his phone, much less asked for his password. But there it was, apparently not password-protected. The caller's name was right there for the world—and her—to see:

DuoMed Aircraft

Why would his old job be calling? He'd been out of there and retired for two years already. Two years, seven months, three weeks and what was it, four days. Every day, for some reason, he'd wake up and recite how long he'd been retired. It was a strange habit, but it must have made him feel good to say it.

She stepped back down into the sunroom. The trees outside were skeletons and a dusting of snow from the other day still clung to the patio. More was supposed to be on the way. But as cold as it was outside, the sun streamed through the wall of windows, warming up the room. The view of a robin's egg sky was stunning.

"Hun. It looks like work is calling you?"

"Thanks, I'll take it." Eric smiled pleasantly. He noticed she had the orange envelope and the papers in her hand. He gave her a thumbs-up with a silly grin. She smiled back and nodded.

"One minute," he mouthed. And then, into his phone, he said, "Hello?"

He started back into the house, squeezing her shoulder as he passed by. Then he paced around the kitchen, circling the center island and tapping the faucet each time with three fingers.

"Oh yes....no...not a problem. Thanks for letting me know."

He got off and his eyes were wide. "Well, that was a surprise."

"What's that?" She hoped it wasn't bad news.

"That 401K, for some reason, they'd split it into a main account and a smaller account. They called to say I could combine them if I wanted to. I told them yes."

"Now? After more than two years? Who the hell is their benefits person, Rip van Winkle?"

He smiled. "You know, just DuoMed folks being their usual inefficient selves."

"What's in the accounts now?"

He scratched his chin. "The big one, you know, that's the one that always makes money somehow. Maybe eight hundred thou. The other, only about thirty-five hundred. So yeah, I told them to send me the form by email and I'll just do an electronic signature. Strange that they never mentioned it before."

"That is strange. Well, a few extra thousand we didn't know about. Not a bad piece of news."

"Absolutely, my love. So that cruise, huh! Looking forward to it?" He walked back into the sunroom.

"You betcha." Then she thought for a minute. "I'll bring your phone back to the breakfront since I'm going inside to put the cruise stuff back on the tray."

"Sure. Thanks."

The screen was still active when she took the phone. She passed the foyer and headed for the bedroom, trying not to look like she was hurrying. With Eric happily ensconced on the loveseat and his nose in a magazine, she snuck a look at the number and memorized it. With that, the screen faded and the phone went black.

She replaced it in the tray, then got a pen and a sticky note and scribbled it down.

Rozina hated feeling suspicious. Why, after so many years in a loving, if somewhat predictable, marriage, had she suddenly become wary?

She thought about her recent therapy session. Sandra said maybe she was feeling unsettled because they were crossing a threshold, with Rozina retiring and facing the rest of her life with somebody who, at times, she'd been too busy (they'd been too busy) to continue exploring. "It happens to all couples," she told Rozina. "A new stage of life is a very natural time to re-examine your relationship and your place and role, not just in the marriage but in terms of how you fit in the world right now."

Rozina had understood, but it was curious that she was even thinking about that strange call he'd gotten.

"I'm going to drop off these supplies to the animal shelter. Want to come along?" she called to Eric.

"No thanks. Let's take a walk to Coney Island Avenue when you get back, okay? The farmer's market runs all day. I'd much rather go today than tomorrow. Saturdays are too busy."

Eric loved to get to the farmer's market early for the apple turnovers, but seeing as Rozina was going out, he could always get the less popular raspberry or lemon custard. It wouldn't take long for her to go to the shelter, but it was enough time for him to finish repainting the last of the lead soldiers with rifles. There were twenty in all, some standing with their rifles pointing to the sky, some sighting them, some lying on the ground. He'd used up most of the dark blue paint and only half the red was left, which he notated in his ledger. As soon as there were enough supplies on the list to get a discount, he'd place the order.

Pretty soon, Eric would take a full inventory of what he'd accomplished and get ready to sell all the figurines. Considering he'd picked up most of them at garage and estate sales for peanuts, he made a great profit that more than paid for his hobby.

Rozina could smell the acrylic paints. She was genuinely happy to see him get so much pleasure from his hobbies, and now that he was occupied, he wouldn't be watching the clock and hurrying her to come home. She packed the trunk with all the items she was donating to the shelter for the month: sheets, cleaning supplies, dog cookies and kitty litter. Her senior discount sure came in handy.

The shelter was a fifteen-minute drive over to Flatbush Avenue. Parking would be a bear. It would take three or four trips with her dolly to drop everything off. She might even sneak in a cupcake at one of those hippy-dippy stores and enjoy it in her car with the music turned on before heading back home. After dropping off the supplies and making a quick phone call, she'd welcome a little solitude. Perhaps today, she would finally try their cappuccino cupcake.

Rozina found a spot on a side street and pulled in, switching off the ignition. Her heart was pumping harder as she knew what she had to do first.

"DuoMed Incorporated. Please hold."

She drummed her fingers on the dashboard, nervous about what was coming.

"DuoMed. How can I help you?"

"Hi, we just got a call from the R&D Division and...."

"Transferring."

She had rehearsed her spiel. She was ready.

"R&D, Berrington speaking."

"Hi, this is...this is Rozina DuPont. My husband Eric just received a call and we didn't get a chance to call back."

"Oh yeah! Rick! How is he?"

Rick?

"Just loving retirement! And that's why I'm calling. Is there anything we need to do with that fund?"

"What fund?"

She took a beat. "Oh, I just thought...."

"Oh, you mean the pensions? Yeah, they took a little hit, but they'll bounce back. They always do. We were actually calling to make sure he knew about the investigation."

Another beat. "The one about...?"

This guy sounded awfully cheerful for an investigation going on.

"Oh yeah. He said it was fine and didn't matter. I guess he didn't tell you. Don't worry, my wife and I don't communicate either. Ha! By the way, I'm Charlie Berrington."

The name was familiar. Eric worked in purchasing and didn't have too much to do with R&D, but he might have mentioned a Charlie.

Rozina cleared her throat. “Right. So the investigation, I just wanted to give him whatever updates you might have. He got off the phone so quick, I found it hard to believe he really listened.” She was winging it.

“Oh yeah. So that sax player who ‘fell’ off the Verrazano, he tested positive for a chemical we use here all the time. It’s pretty rare, though. The cops were trying to find out if anybody had access to it, and so I was just telling Rick to expect a call in case they were going to question our former employees and anyone who recently retired.”

Her brain froze.

“Mrs. DuPont?”

“Oh yes, sorry. So no, I mean, he’s been retired for two years now.” And seven months and three weeks.

Charlie gave a loud laugh. “You don’t have to convince me of anything! Hey, so what’s he been up to? Still painting those antique toy soldiers?”

That, and maybe some other stuff I don’t know about.

The last thing Jerry Zolotov felt as his body slammed into the Verrazano Narrows was his saxophone crashing into his skull. The body was retrieved three days later. It had washed up at a picnic area off the Palisades side of the Narrows. A seven-year-old who was flying a kite with his father was the first to see it. He didn't speak for months afterward.

Toxicology found a trace of pentium phosphorus in Jerry's system. No alcohol, no vitamins, no supplements, no hormones, nothing out of whack. The sole exception was the poison. The technician said it was most likely soaked into the reed that Jerry licked right before he slid it onto his ligature, causing him to be stricken with vertigo and an intractable migraine. He lost his footing on the slick surface, grabbed for the railing, and missed, going over into the turbulent waters below. The only way they knew how the fatal substance was administered was by examining the extra reeds still in plastic wrappers in his case. They were zipped up inside an old bank deposit pouch that Jerry must have forgotten he had when he used his worn-out reed.

Toxicology examined the wrappers under a microscope and noticed they'd been tampered with through injection, evidenced by tiny punctures near the crimp of the packaging. Unfortunately for the investigation, there were a lot of sources for the extra-fine needles that could have delivered the poison.

The cause of death was officially listed as lethal fall (primary) and poisoning (secondary). All that remained to be determined was identifying who could have had access to the toxin itself, which was almost impossible to come by; however, not rare in the aerospace industry.

Eric looked appreciatively at his wife as she emerged from the warm Florida Panhandle waters. At sixty-seven years old, Rozina still had a great body. Sure, the signs of age were there, but she looked healthy and fit. She was finally happy. Stress-free. No work, no commitments, a time to relax and enjoy the golden years in front of them.

Moving south was the perfect next step in their lives. And now that she was officially retired, she could spend her days enjoying quiet, carefree days of fresh-caught shrimp and having a glass of something bold and red each night for the rest of her days with the man she loved, without having to worry anymore about a demanding job or a boss who had wild mood swings. It wasn't the way she wanted things to turn out, but life was short, made painfully obvious by the tragic end that befell Jerry. It was important to embrace every minute.

She smoothed her silver hair back and fixed the strap on her right shoulder that had settled on her upper arm. She caught Eric's eye and smiled at him. He returned a sultry look.

It was a beautiful thing to see Rozina so relaxed and finally enjoying life, he mused. It had taken a while to get here, but once he figured things out, it was quite simple, really. All it took was access to a saxophone named Violet and a little poison.

Debbie Burke is an award-winning author of nine books, including the jazz novels *Icarus Flies Home* and *Glissando: A Story of Love, Lust and Jazz*, and the interview series *Tasty Jazz Jams for Our Times*. She launched her internationally acclaimed jazz blog debbieburkeauthor.com in 2016 and her editing/author coaching business, Queen Esther Publishing LLC, in 2020. Brooklyn-born, she has lived in six different states in the eastern half of the US but most of all, loves being near the ocean. When she isn't writing, she's learning new licks on the sax.

Also by Debbie Burke

FICTION

Glissando: A Story of Love, Lust and Jazz
Icarus Flies Home

NONFICTION

Tasty Jazz Jams for Our Times, Vol. 1 and Vol. 2
Klezmer for the Joyful Soul
The Poconos in B Flat
The Author's Little Red Guide to Editing
Music in the Scriptures

Please leave a review of this book on Amazon at https://bit.ly/DebbieBurkeAmazon. Thank you!

Made in the USA
Middletown, DE
23 December 2022